Praise for "]

"This book had me laughing, crying, falling in love, and everything in between. A wild sexy ride! Steamy, funny, and down to earth—what more can you ask for?"

— Lyna Smith

Evie's haven is a small-town romance with a sweet innocence about it. Sweet with a dash of spice.... She's just getting back into the dating scene after heartbreaking loss. I really liked Evie's open demeanour and I was really rooting for her in her journey to finding love again.

The writing is great, and the female friendships are well-developed. Evie's relationship with her daughter is especially heartwarming.

— Kate Smidts

Funny and heartfelt... The main characters are refreshingly real, with lots of playful banter, thoughtful moments, and sexy fun! This debut novel is deeply satisfying and will leave you wanting more!

— Luanne Pyper Voisin

Evie's Haven

Evie's Haven

Lisa Plaice

Land Acknowledgment

Storeylines Press operates on the lands of the Anishinabek, Haudenosauneega Confederacy, and Anishinaabe, Treaty 29, 1827. As settlers to this area, we acknowledge the rights and importance of the Indigenous people and their importance to this region, nation, and its culture, as well as their unjust treatment by the Canadian government and settlers past and present.

*This book is dedicated to the memory of
my grandmother, Evelyn,
who was an avid romance reader.*

Contents

Chapter One

"Come on, baby, give Mama what she wants."

My coffee maker was old, really old. And apparently it needed the water filter changed out quite badly. I had ordered a new package of filters online last week. Unfortunately, I'd received an email yesterday informing me that they were back-ordered. That meant that I was going to have to make it through just a few more days with this old clogged one.

I stood hunched over the kitchen counter with my head resting in my hands, watching the coffee slowly, achingly begin to drip into the pot.

"Now that's what I'm talking about!"

Coffee, the sweet nectar of the gods. Now, being that I own a café, I suppose I could just wait for my caffeine fix until I got to work. But there was one problem with that: How would I get to work without first waking up? I was feeling blurry-eyed and cranky. But in my defence, it was only four forty-five in the morning. It is also very important that I arrive at work with my clothes on the right way around. Sadly, that was not an example of how tired I am that just popped into my brain, but an actual memory. However, that had been John's fault for bringing home decaffeinated coffee and emptying it into the decorative canister, all without noticing the word 'Decaffeinated' on the label. I mean, don't people want me to maintain my 'no violence committed due to lack of caffeine' streak?

At last there was just enough coffee for me to pour myself a cup. Cradling it like a precious baby, I headed back upstairs to get ready for work. As I passed my daughter Sara's room, I made sure to tip-toe. I might have to be up this early, but Sara—at eighteen and in her last year of high school—did not. Although Sara got herself up and ready for school long after I had left for the café, I still liked to drive her to school myself. It was usually something that I would come back to the house to do after Katie, my employee and one of my best friends, started for the day.

Once back in my room, I brushed the knots out of my hair and began to get dressed, all while inhaling great gulps of coffee. I decided today would be a good day to try out my new silk scarf. Katie always makes fun of how I dress. "Too fancy for café folks." But I dressed to please myself, and I could always cover the scarf up with my apron while baking. I looked longingly at my new high-heeled boots sitting in the corner of my room, begging to be worn. *A bridge too far, Evie,* I told myself, *a bridge too far.*

Even though I love to sleep in, I also loved serving all

in-house baked goodies at my café. I truly enjoyed baking all the muffins, cookies, and squares from scratch. Most of the recipes were from my mother's cookbook, handwritten in her beautiful cursive writing. I loved letting my creativity flow in the kitchen, tweaking her recipes to suit my mood or the availability of fresh seasonal ingredients.

Katie had volunteered to come in early every other day to do the baking, now that her youngest was in a full-day, every-other-day kindergarten. But I told her to sleep in. With three kids, all under twelve, I figured she needed all the extra sleep she could get.

Besides, since John died, I always seemed to wake up early, and I never seemed able to get back to sleep. I figured the early shift really seemed to suit me anyway.

My café, which I named *The Princesses Café*, is located in an ancient building on Main Street in Haven, my hometown. The sign hanging above the door had a huge, ornate golden crown, and the scrolled lettering was set inside it. The building itself definitely had its quirks. The front door would always stick in the summer. The air conditioning worked well, but the heating... not so much. It was lucky that I did all my own baking, because at least that helped boost the furnace in the cold weather a bit.

My landlord was a nice enough fellow but, to quote him, 'I just don't have it in the budget for a new furnace right now.' That quote was from five years ago. Oh well, that just meant that I would haul out the little electric heater on frigid days. Luckily, electricity was included in my rent.

3

. . .

I WAS ON A ROLL TODAY; I had accomplished all the cookies, muffins, and squares by the time Katie walked in the door at seven forty-five. I even had enough extra time to make something new: gingerbread squares, which I would serve warm, topped with real whipped cream.

"Something smells very good in here, very... pumpkin latte."

"Yes, even though gingerbread is usually a fall thing, I suddenly had a craving. I'm hoping it will go over well with the regulars."

Katie threw her purse on the table in the back room and put her apron on.

"Don't you have to go?"

"Oh, Sara. Just let me grab my phone. I will tell her to be ready for me on the front porch."

Sara answered on the first ring.

"Mom, I don't need a ride." But she pronounced the word need, like 'neeeed.' "I have Olivia coming to pick me up any minute. I told you that last night."

"I don't remember you telling me that."

"Well, I did. I'm pretty sure that I did. And... even if I didn't, I have told you a million times that I don't need a ride. Now, please stop fussing."

"How long has Olivia had her license?"

"For a year and a half, and no accidents. Now please, I've got to go. She's honking her horn outside for me. We're leaving early to get lattes on our way to school."

"Lattes? I guess I will see you soon then."

"No, you won't. We aren't coming to the café for our

4

lattes. You would probably make Olivia show you her driver's license or check her insurance. Got to go, Mom, bye."

And with that, the phone went dead. "Bye then," I said to myself.

Katie popped her head around the corner. "You couldn't help me for a couple of minutes before you go get Sara, could you?" She gave me her hopeful look, complete with a tilted head and colossal puppy-dog eyes.

"I can help you out for all sorts of minutes. As a matter of fact, Sara doesn't need a ride. Well... not from me anyway."

"Thank God. Sorry, but all of a sudden, I am swamped out there."

I pulled my new silk scarf out of my apron and quickly retied it around my neck.

HALF AN HOUR LATER, Katie got that mischievous smile on her face. She leaned in towards me and whispered, "Well, well, well, look who's here." I looked up towards the door as a good-looking man in a red shirt came in. "You know, he always asks for you when he comes in. I think he has the hots for you."

He had reached the counter by this point and smiled at me as if he had just won the lotto.

"Evelyn, so nice to see you."

"You can call me Evie. Everyone does."

"Oh, Evie. Sorry about that. I didn't mean to seem so formal. You look so pretty today. That scarf with all the flowers . . . It suits you... very spring." He was sweating a little and seemed nervous.

"Thank you so much... It's new." I reached up and touched it, suddenly self-conscious. "Can I help you? Coffee, I'm assuming. And you take it black, if I remember correctly."

"Yes, thanks. You remembered my order. I feel special."

He smiled again as I handed him his coffee. "Speaking of special, I have a new special today. Warmed gingerbread squares topped with real whipped cream."

"Well, if you made them, then yes. Everything you bake is always so delicious."

As I rang up his total, I saw Katie pretending to restock the cups. Cups that clearly didn't need restocking. She had that look on her face, like she was barely holding in a laugh, and as soon as he left the counter, Katie almost skipped over.

"Somebody's got a boyfriend," she sang right into my ear. "Go on... tell me his nickname. You have to have come up with one for him. Lay it on me."

"Ernest," I said quietly.

"No, not his real name. His nickname."

"His nickname is Ernest. Because... because he is just so... so earnest. His real name is Charles, by the way."

"Oh, that's so sweet. So, you like this one? Finally, after all the good-looking men I've pointed out to you. Men that you have nit-picked and made up excuses not to go after. Finally!"

"You can stop celebrating," I said as I turned to wipe the counter. "I am not going to date Ernest, er... Charles."

"Why? He obviously likes you. And he is so sweet."
As she said that, I turned to look at him sitting at his table
and found him staring at me. When our eyes met, he
gave me the thumbs-up signal and pointed to his
gingerbread square. I smiled back at him and turned
around to face Katie.

"I am not ready to date... yet. And you know that.
Besides, even if I was ready—which I am *not*—I don't feel
any sparks with him. He's a good-looking guy and, like
you said, sweet. But no sparks."

"You never even give these guys a chance to create
any sparks. You are way too busy throwing cold water all
over any hint of sparks. You know... if you always insist
on playing it safe and never take any risks, you might
miss out on something wonderful."

I was just about to come up with my reasons why
playing it safe was the most reasonable thing to do when
my phone rang.

"Mrs. Jones?" the voice through the phone asked.

"Yes, this is her. I mean, that's me." My mind was
suddenly swimming. My brain was telling me I had
forgotten something. But what?

"Mrs. Jones, this is Ryan, the contractor you spoke to
last week. We had a meeting set up at ten o'clock this
morning. I'm standing on your front porch, but no one
seems to be home."

Bingo. That's why those alarm bells had been ringing
in my head. This was so unlike me, to forget a meeting I
had just recently set up.

"I am so sorry. I completely forgot. I can be there in

five minutes," I said as I threw on my coat and grabbed my purse.

"Sorry," I mouthed to Katie, who was busy helping a customer. "Got to go." She waved at me and continued assisting the customer without skipping a beat.

I PULLED into my driveway to find a large blue pickup truck in front of the house with the logo **Sullivan Contracting** written on the side in bold black letters. The owner of that truck currently sat on my front porch swing. He stood up as I bounded up the steps, breathing heavily. He was a very attractive-looking man with a tall, muscular build and a stellar smile. Dark brown hair that he kept short and a well-trimmed beard. Forty? I guessed. Maybe a little younger. He smiled at me again and held out his hand.

"Hello. Nice to meet you, Mrs. Jones. I'm Ryan. We spoke last week about me coming to your house today to give you a quote on finishing your basement."

I shook his hand and just hoped that mine wasn't sweaty. "Evie," I said. "You can call me Evie, and yes, we did speak about this last week. Again, I am so sorry to have forgotten about you." I fumbled with the front door's passcode and held the door open for Ryan to come in.

"You have a beautiful home." Ryan had taken off his boots and looked around the front hall appreciatively.

"Thank you." And suddenly I realized that some time must have gone by and I had been standing there just staring at him. Worse than that, I think he might have just asked me a question.

"Sorry, can you repeat that?" *I mean, seriously, Evie? Get it together!* What must the man think of me? First, I forget about him and leave him standing on my front porch, and then when I finally arrive... I stare at him like an idiot.

"I said that you must not have been far away because you really did get here in five minutes."

"Yes, I was at work at my café on Main Street" *There. See, Evie, you can answer a question without looking like a flustered fool.*

"Oh, do you own The Princesses Café, by any chance? I have not had the pleasure of trying it out. But my sister raves about it."

"Oh, well then... your sister obviously has good taste." I gave him a cheeky smile.

He smiled. "Perhaps you could show me the way to the basement? I will get working on that quote for you."

Chapter Two

The door to the basement was in the front hall. The in-law suite I hoped to build would share a common front hall. That way, the house and the apartment could share the laundry and powder rooms. A sizeable French door, which could itself be locked, separated the front hall from the main house. This way, the doors would be closed and locked if the apartment were simply a rental property. But if other family members were using it, then the doors could all stay open, and the family could flow through the house as they wished.

We had partially finished the stairway down to the basement with drywall, but little else had been done. Once downstairs, you could see the framing that had been started.

John had made finishing the basement his project before he got sick. He wasn't put off by the amount of work or the fact that he had never done anything like that before. John had been a lawyer and a damned good one. Carpentry wasn't exactly in his wheelhouse, so to speak. But he said that he liked the idea of poking away at the basement, and he joked that he hoped the work would give him some "manly calluses." He seemed to really enjoy his time working with his hands. But now the sight of the partially finished and abandoned framing made my stomach squeeze a little, and suddenly I felt slightly sick.

"Well, someone started this job for me. I can see the outline of the rooms that have been set out." Ryan walked around the basement, looking at and touching the wood framing. "This is obviously the bathroom... the bedroom... the living room... and I'm guessing this is the open-concept kitchen?"

"That's correct, and we were also thinking of finishing the area under the stairs as a closet and some general storage space."

"We? You and your husband or partner? Is he the handyman that started this work?"

"Yes, John, my husband. He was working on finishing the basement. It was his project in his spare time."

"Was? Did he get in over his head? Or maybe he just got too busy with his other job?"

"John passed away three years ago."

"I am so sorry for your loss. My condolences." He looked at me with large, soulful eyes, and when he made eye contact, he didn't seem to feel uncomfortable with the situation at all. It was comforting to see empathy and not sense an internal struggle to get away from this awkward conversation.

"Thank you. John and I always thought that completing an in-law suite could add to the value of our home. And that it would help sell the house to a larger demographic of people when the time came."

"I agree." Ryan nodded. "A larger house like this one, in this housing market, would be affordable to a lot more people with a built-in mortgage helper. Why don't I come up with a plan for this project? With a few different levels of finishes and the corresponding quotes? That way, if you are happy with one of the quotes, you can call me, and we will see about signing the paperwork and firming up a start date." With that, he produced a business card.

As I watched Ryan's truck pull away, I sighed and blew out a breath I didn't realize I had been holding onto. *I am going to do this,* I lectured myself. *I am going to finish your work, John. I will get an excellent price for our house, and then I will downsize with Sara into one of those lovely condos they will soon start building on First Street. Life is going to be so much more manageable after that. I will begin to feel like I have my feet under me again, I just know it.*

THE REST of the day passed in a blur. The café was busy all day, and my gingerbread squares were a hit. They sold out just before the lunchtime crowd. Suddenly, Sandy appeared at the counter.

"Is it that time of day already?" I asked her." I have completely lost track of time. I haven't even packaged up the leftovers yet."

Sandy came from Haven's Food Bank every evening to collect unsold baked goods.

"Oh, Evie! You know that you don't have to package them yourself."

"It's no problem. I like doing it, and especially adding my Princesses sticker. I think that it makes the cookie or muffin feel more like a treat, just for them. Besides, you have probably been on your feet all day. Have a seat, and I will bring you over a coffee to keep you occupied while I quickly package up this lot." I gathered up all my unsold goodies and headed to the kitchen.

Sandy looked a lot like her name, I thought. Sandy light brown hair and dark brown eyes. She was taller than the average woman but, at the same time, seemed rather delicate. Sandy had become a nightly fixture in the café—I could almost set my watch by her. She has run Haven's Food Bank for a few years now, and since then, she has cultivated a good relationship with many local shops. l knew of the local family-run bakery, the deli across the street, and one small family-owned grocery store that, in addition to my café, she was able to gather up donations of food from. Food that might have otherwise ended up in the garbage. It was a lot of extra work for Sandy, but she always seemed to put the Food Bank ahead of her personal time. She said that she didn't mind putting in the extra effort, and she always seemed to have a smile on her face.

As I put a sticker on the last of the packaged cookies. I could overhear Katie talking to Sandy. "Ernest" was all I could make out, but that was enough.

"Stop gossiping about nonexistent relationships,

Katie! Sandy is a busy woman, and you should be on your way home to that gorgeous hubby of yours and those three little angels. Now shoo!"

Sandy stage-whispered to Katie, "Oh, the lady doth protest too much, methinks... You might be right about this Ernest fellow." Sandy then winked conspiratorially at Katie, and they both started laughing.

"All right... both of you, out! You are both well aware that I am much too busy with my life to add dating Ernest... ugh... Charles or anyone else into the mix. I have Sara waiting for acceptance letters from three universities, I'm running this place, and now I'm renovating my basement. Besides, I was fortunate to have already had the love of my life."

Katie was pulling her coat on and grabbing her gigantic purse. Seriously, gigantic... I mean, what in the world does she keep in there?

"Oh, how exciting." Sandy said, "Where are these universities located? Anywhere close by?"

"Yes, there are two excellent universities with Psychology programs within forty-five minutes of here. And then there is the University of British Columbia. But, let's face it, she isn't going to go there. It is just too far away."

"Oh, I don't know about that," Sandy said as she packed all the individually sealed goodies into a cardboard box. "When I was her age, I got into the local university and a university five hours away. I chose the university that was five hours away... because... well, because it was five hours away from my parents. It was so exciting to be on my own, away from home. Just the freedom of it. I actually think that's pretty normal."

"Yes," I said. "I can see what you're saying. But that's just not Sara and me. Since John died, we are all we have left and we are very close. She would never want to go so far away from home."

I held the door open for Sandy to leave with the large box of packaged goodies in her hands. Katie followed, locking the door behind us.

"I'm sure that you are right about Sara." Sandy huffed as she reshuffled the box. "I was known to be a little wild at her age."

I HAD DECIDED to be a little naughty and pick up takeout for supper. Sara and I could have a girl's night. Fast food in front of the TV watching a scary movie. With a big-girl glass of cold white wine for myself, and for Sara, her favourite grape-flavoured pop. I think I might even break into my emergency chocolate stash. Maybe do each other's nails?

Winter was finally losing its grip on Haven. So I was enjoying the breeze through the car and drove all the way home with the windows down. It was a little cold, and... it probably wasn't doing anything good for the burgers and fries. But I was too busy enjoying the first hint of spring in the air.

When I opened the front door, the house was silent. The kind of silence that settles into your bones. Even though John had been gone for years now, I would still find myself expecting to hear him yell "I'm in here!" from the living room when I walked through the front door.

My phone chirped with the sound of a text coming in. It was Sara.

'Back by 10... invited to Olivia's Mom's house for supper... having fondue and watching a movie.' A smiley face emoji followed this.

I had forgotten to check in with Sara. Ugh. I had just assumed that she would be free. Wow, that was stupid! What the hell am I going to do with an extra burger and fries? Scratch that. I would *definitely* eat the extra fries—let's get real.

Suddenly my evening yawned in front of me. And, in the end, I just decided to get into my pyjamas and eat supper sitting propped up with pillows in my bed. I was re-watching my favourite British murder mystery series and I had already watched all the episodes twice. I found it comforting to rewatch my favourite shows when I was feeling down. It took very little mental energy, so I could zone out from time to time and still know exactly what was happening in the show.

I managed to stay awake long enough to see Sara arrive home safe and sound. Then I set the sleep timer on the TV for thirty minutes—I was fast asleep before it turned itself off.

Chapter Three

I woke up Monday morning without needing an alarm clock at four. But I didn't need to be up quite that early. I decided that, since I would never be able to get back to sleep, I might as well head to work and get an early start on my baking for Saturday. I bake enough goodies for Saturday ahead of time and then freeze them. This way, my two weekend employees could have freshly baked products to sell just by thawing them an hour or so before opening. Well, basically fresh. I liked to do my own baking, but I definitely want to have my Saturdays off!

It was freezing in the café, so I decided to keep my winter hat on while the ovens heated up. That was this time of year for you: spring one minute and back to the heart of winter the next.

Katie arrived, looking tired. She explained that her youngest had some kind of stomach flu, and she had been up several times through the night. I was just about to tell her to go home and go back to bed when I remembered that the workers were coming to the house to start the renovations today.

"Katie, I have to get back to the house to let the workers in and go over a few things with them. Oh... and then drive Sara to school. But when I get back, you can clock out early and go back to bed."

"I'm fine, don't worry. I can work my usual hours. My hubby is off today. Besides, I wouldn't get much sleep with a sick and very cranky four-year-old around." Katie stifled a yawn and then smiled sleepily.

I ENDED up wasting a lot of time trying in vain to find my hat. It was still on my head, and in the process of looking, I was late for Ryan and his men again. Should I explain that I was running around the back of the café for ten minutes looking for my hat? The hat on my head? That would probably not help my case. Instead of being a lady that can't keep time... I would be a ditzy lady that can't keep time.

Sure enough, Ryan was once again sitting on my front porch. Two of his men had set out a myriad of supplies on my driveway. They were currently standing by their pickup truck and drinking coffee in takeout cups that came from a fast-food restaurant.

"I'm so sorry. What must you think of me?" I said as I carefully hopscotched around the equipment on the driveway. "But I will make up for it tomorrow. I'll bring you guys a really nice coffee from my café. Or a cappuccino, or a latte, if you prefer."

Ryan's men laughed and told me that it was much appreciated, but two black coffees would be great. I ran up the front steps, and Ryan stood up from the swing.

"Does that coffee offer extend to me?" He smiled, and the corners of his dark eyes crinkled. "I won't be here tomorrow, but could I stop by the café and maybe do some of my paperwork there? With a cappuccino? I have never tried a cappuccino."

Suddenly I felt hot and flustered. Was I blushing? I certainly hope not! Why was I getting so nervous around this man?

"Of course. I will even throw in a muffin. I mean, this is the second time that I have kept you waiting on my front porch."

"Don't worry about it," he said as he held my front door open for his men to start bringing in the equipment. At that very moment, Sara ran out the door while simultaneously struggling to get her backpack on.

"Bye, Mom! Got to go... Olivia just pulled up."

"But... I can drive you. I just needed to let the men in, and then I can come right back after I drop you off."

"It's okay, Mom. I like driving in with Olivia. I get to catch up on all the gossip on the drive."

"Well, tell her to watch her speed at First Street. There is a new pothole there, and I don't want her swerving around it and maybe getting into an accident."

"You worry too much, Mom. I'll see you tonight. Don't forget—I have a shift at the drugstore after school, so I won't be home till seven for supper." And with that, she disappeared down the driveway, almost colliding with one of the men.

21

"How old?" Ryan asked, following me to the basement stairs.

"Eighteen. It feels funny even to say that my baby is eighteen."

"She looks just like you."

"Yes, she does, doesn't she? Although she has her father's fair colouring." I twisted my brown hair around my finger. John had blond hair and the most beautiful blue eyes, kind of like looking at the sky.

After the equipment was all unloaded by Ryan and his two men, they headed down to the basement. The two men consisted of David, the younger of the two and still in his apprenticeship, and Paul, the more experienced. I guessed him to be around my age. Forty-five? It was hard to tell just from looking. Ryan ran through the basic layout of the framing to be started and then turned back to me.

"I told you in the quote that there are three different choices of finishes in total. You signed off on the basic level package. I still need to go through the other two levels with you. They are an additional cost, but many of my customers have felt that the extra money was well worth it."

"Yes, I would like to see some samples or pictures of the choices."

"Well, why don't I stop by the café tomorrow for my free cappuccino and muffin? I'll bring some samples, and I can show you some examples on my laptop."

"Sounds good. I guess I will see you tomorrow." And, with that, he was gone, and I was left with a nervous stomach, thinking about tomorrow.

. . .

TUESDAY MORNING ENDED up being busier than usual. I think that the distraction was a blessing in more ways than just financial. My mind kept wandering back to thinking about Ryan coming in today. Katie kept catching me fussing with my new silk blouse or brushing flour off my face in the reflection of the toaster.

"I said it before, and I will say it again... I don't know why you wear such fancy clothes to work." Katie reached forward to brush a spot of dried dough from this morning's baking off my shoulder.

"It's not that fancy. And it has sat in my drawer unworn for over six months now. I cut the tags off it this morning. Besides, if I don't wear it to work, then where am I going to wear it?"

Katie was busy refilling the grinder with coffee beans. "Maybe... if you went on a date?" she said, turning to look at me. "You know, like, maybe with one of the many handsome men that I have pointed out to you? That seems like a much better fit for a beautiful new black silk blouse. Don't you think?"

"As I've told you so many—" I started, but movement near the counter caught my eye. It was Mike; he had become a recent fixture in the café. Coming in every Tuesday, Wednesday, and Thursday. Where did he go on Mondays and Fridays, I wondered. Katie gave me the side eye the entire time I filled Mike's order. When he walked away, Katie rushed over and whispered emphatically in my ear.

"Well... what about him? Now he has some new-blouse-wearing potential. He is handsome and very fit, and I think he is interested in you."

"Why do you think that?"

"I overheard him ask you last Thursday if you had any plans for the weekend."

"So what? That is called small talk, Katie."

"No. That is called fishing, Evie."

"Well, in that case, this fish isn't biting." I turned and walked away from Katie and began to rearrange the muffins in the antique glass display case.

"Come on, lay it on me. What's his name?"

"Birth control," I whispered just loud enough for Katie to hear.

"Ohhhh... I get it. Because he is so sexy, you would need lots?" Katie winked and smiled while pointing to her head.

"No. Because his breath is so bad it should be considered birth control."

We then began to laugh until tears rolled down our faces. And it was while wiping tears away that I saw Ryan standing at the counter in front of me.

"Ryan," I said while trying to control myself. "What can I get you? Oh yes... You said that you wanted to try a cappuccino, right?"

"Yes, that would be great," Ryan said as he looked back and forth between Katie and me. "Do you two always have so much fun at work? Maybe I'm in the wrong profession?"

If Katie hadn't been such a talented barista, she would have made an outstanding detective. "So, Ryan..." she said, zeroing in on him. "Evie has talked you into trying a cappuccino. Do you think you would like to try it with extra foam? Or maybe with a double shot of espresso?" She was looking suspiciously between the two of us.

"I don't know. I've never tried one before. But when Evie mentioned it yesterday... I thought it was about time that I did. Maybe just one shot of espresso, though. Too much caffeine makes me jittery. Thanks."

Katie was now grinding the espresso beans while simultaneously observing Ryan and me carefully.

"Oh, I almost forgot. What about the muffin I promised you? What kind would you like?"

"What kind do you recommend?"

"I just came up with a new muffin today. It's a strawberry muffin with fresh mint and white chocolate chunks. I call it the Spring Fling muffin."

"That sounds interesting. I think I will try one of those."

Katie was back with Ryan's cappuccino, and it did not escape my notice that she had made a large heart in the middle of the foam. With a smaller trail of hearts that encircled the edge of the cup.

"I am sure you are busy, Evie," Ryan said. "But I am going to get set up with my laptop and the samples that I brought, over there at that larger table." He gestured with his head, his hands full. "And you can join me whenever you are free."

Katie waited until he was out of earshot.

"Oh, join him, Evie. Join him." She was hopping and doing that tiny little excited clap.

"Before you get the wrong idea, that"—I pointed

vaguely under the counter toward him—"is Ryan, my contractor. You know, the contractor that I hired to finish my basement?"

Katie's smug little smile was growing. "Tell me more," she said, her voice low and deep.

"Stop that." I playfully swatted her arm. "Ryan is here to show me a couple of different up-sell levels of finishing for the basement. You know, like wainscotting and different styles of doors. And, you know... knobs and stuff like that."

Katie cocked her head to one side and put a finger on her chin. "Oh. I get it. So what you are saying? Correct me if I'm wrong, but you're saying... that he wants to show you his knob?"

"Ugh. I give up. I am not speaking with you about this. You have such a dirty mind." I reached around my back to untie my apron. As I walked around the counter, I heard Katie whisper.

"You never know. You might just like Ryan's knob. If you ever let him get close enough to be able to show you."

I'm sure that I am blushing now. Well, here goes nothing. I mean... what? I am simply being shown upgrades for the basement. Why was I feeling nervous about that? But my mind kept coming back to the knobs. Knobs. Knobs... stop it. Bad brain! When I arrived at the table, Ryan looked up from setting out his samples.

"Oh, hi again," he said. "Your face is flushed. Are you feeling alright?"

"I'm fine. Just fine... great, in fact. I mean, it's just working back in the kitchen with all those hot ovens." Damn, I was good!

"Of course. Please have a seat, and I'll take you through the other two levels of finishes. First on the computer, and then you can handle any or all of the samples."

Like your knob? Brain! Stop that!

FORTY-FIVE MINUTES LATER, I had decided on the second level of upgrade finishes. And I was very impressed with Ryan's presentation. He had done a computer mock-up of my basement and was able to show me onscreen exactly what my basement would look like, with all three levels of finishings. And... most importantly... I managed to do it without blushing or thinking about his knob! Knob. Ugh... Katie!

WHEN I GOT HOME after closing up the café, the men were gone. I had set up a temporary code for them on my front door keypad. That allowed them to come and go as needed while I was at work. I still liked seeing them when they arrived in the morning. I found that it was an excellent time to get caught up on their progress and to answer any questions that might have come up.

David and Paul had been quite busy today. The framing was well on its way. While I was poking around, admiring the framing, I heard footsteps overhead.

"Sara? Come down here, please!" I yelled up the stairs. Sara ran down the stairs. Her long blonde hair was pulled up into that cute messy-bun look that I never seemed able to pull off.

"Wow!" she said as she looked around. "It's so good to see Dad's project going ahead." She smiled sadly and gave me a hug. "Oh, before I forget, I will be out late on Friday night. The cinema is having a showing of the Rocky Horror Picture Show, and Olivia and this new girl, Ann, are coming too. We are going all out with our costumes_it's going to be a riot."

"Okay, sounds like fun. Who is this Ann? Where did you meet her, at work? Or school?"

"Don't worry, Mom. She's new to town, and I met her in my biology class. She ended up sitting near me, and we got to talking. She is pretty cool, actually."

"Is Olivia driving? Or this Ann?"

"Actually, I was just getting to that..." Sara said, her eyes getting bigger. "Could I please have the car for Friday night? Please? Olivia's car is in the shop, and Ann doesn't have her driver's license yet."

"I guess so," I said hesitantly. "But make sure that you are making a full and complete stop at every stop sign. The last time you drove with me, you simply slowed down and looked both ways. We might live in a small town, but that doesn't mean there still aren't other cars on the road."

"Yes, Mom, no problem," Sara said and once again hugged me, more enthusiastically. "Thank you. So much. I will be super careful." And, with that, she ran upstairs.

"Teenagers," I muttered and headed upstairs after her to start supper.

Chapter Four

Y ou could hear the construction noises all the way up the street. As I walked around the corner of First Street, I was absolutely gleeful to see that The Penthouses condo development was finally breaking ground. It was awe-inspiring to watch these enormous machines digging as I stood in front of a full-colour billboard with computer-generated pictures of sample units. There were also examples of some of the extra perks that would come with owning a unit in this prestigious building.

The communal rooftop patio will offer such extras as outdoor pizza ovens, gas BBQs, shaded pergolas, sun loungers, two large all-cedar saunas, and four large year-round-use hot tubs.

Yes, please!

The basement laundry room will be a thing of the past as all units will have their own stackable washer/dryer unit in a laundry room complete with a small sink, shelving, and a stylish built-in drying rack.

Every unit will have a recessed balcony eight feet deep and twenty-two feet wide. This will allow a variety of uses and outdoor furniture placement options. The glass railing will allow for impeccable views of Haven, as well as ensure maximum light into your unit.

A small English-style pub set in the heart of the main lobby will serve on-tap beers and vintage wines from around the world. This pub will be open Friday through Sunday evenings, allowing sports to be viewed on the big screen TVs and serving as a social hub for the condo owners.

The Penthouses. We want to be your home and a part of your community.

I think that I might have been drooling at this point. Yes! Yes, to all of that! I could picture myself having a big glass of wine in the pub with some fellow condo owners on a Friday night and after a long day relaxing with Sara in one of the hot tubs on the rooftop patio. Forget about the saunas, though. Sweating generally just makes me cranky. And cranky me was hardly going to be a popular person to be around while trying to make new friends with my fellow condo owners.

I brought up the subject of The Penthouses with Sara at suppertime. I was excitedly extolling the virtues of the development, and surprised that her level of excitement didn't seem to match my own.

"Sounds great, Mom," she said between bites of her Caesar salad. "It sounds like it will suit you to a T. Especially the fact that it is only two blocks from the café."

"It will be great for you, too," I said. "Just think about how easy it will be for you and me to maintain. No grass to cut, no snow to shovel. And the cleaning time will be cut way back. This house...." I gestured with my fork. "It's just a lot of house for you and me to keep up with. And think about that lovely rooftop patio; you can certainly enjoy that with your girlfriends. It is going to be so easy to be social there."

I looked expectantly over at Sara. But Sara's head was down, looking at her Caesar salad like it suddenly required all her attention.

"It sounds wonderful, Mom. And I am thrilled to hear you're so excited about it. But... you need to remember that I will be busy with school come September. And you know, the possibility exists that I might get into the University of British Columbia, and if that happens... I won't even be living with you. I will be living on the other side of the country." She looked up then and gave me a small smile.

"Sara, I don't even give that idea a second thought.

31

Not with two very good universities with Psychology programs right at our doorstep."

With that, I picked up both our empty plates and placed them in the sink, effectively ending the conversation. Sara came up behind me at the sink and put her arms around my waist, squeezing me tightly with her face buried in my hair.

"It sounds wonderful, Mom," she said quietly and kissed my cheek.

Afterward, Sara helped with the dishes and then disappeared upstairs to do her homework.

I felt restless. After John died, I found that keeping myself busy, distracted had become a coping mechanism that really seemed to help me. But every now and then it failed. It was as if, this evening, I had run out of things to distract myself with. It had begun to rain quite heavily, so taking a walk was out. I knew that Katie was out with her youngest at Mommy and Me gymnastics class, so I couldn't call or ask her to stop by for a glass of wine and a chat. I had finished my library book and hadn't yet made it back to the library to pick a new one. I had just finished binge-watching a Netflix series and was in that post-binge-watching malaise. The one in which you are sad that the series has ended but still unable to muster the energy to start searching for a new one to watch.

I found myself staring out the window at the rain from my favourite spot on the couch, lost in thought. My mind was on John, conjuring him up with me, living at The Penthouses. It was beautiful and, at the same time, achingly sad.

After a while, I realized that it was dark outside. I

was surprised to see how much time had passed, with me lost in my thoughts. Fantasies, really. I got up from the couch and shut the curtains. Then I shut the lights off in the kitchen and headed up the stairs to bed.

THE FOLLOWING DAY, I took extra care with my hair, curling beachy waves with my oversized barrel curling iron. I decided to wear my brand new 'booty-lifting' jeans. At least that was the claim they made. But I had a lot of booty to lift, so gravity-defying was still unlikely.

Ryan had called and left a message to let me know he would be at the house today, as he was bringing in his electrician to run through the job now that the framing was almost finished. He didn't say that I needed to be there. But I always brought Dave and Paul a real coffee from my café when I met with them each morning to run through the expected work for the day. So today I figured I would bring four coffees back with me. No, scratch that... three coffees and one cappuccino. Ryan had enjoyed that one he had tried at the café.

And my booty-lifting jeans and beachy waved hair had nothing to do with Ryan being there today. I like to look nice just for myself, thank you very much! But Katie definitely noticed the extra effort I had put into my appearance today.

"Va-va-va-voom!" She laughed as she took off her coat. "Someone is dressed to impress. But whom, I wonder?" She smiled sweetly at me.

"Oh, just someone smart and incredibly good-looking." I looked dreamily back at her.

"Oh... tell me more," Katie said excitedly. "Who is this smart, hunky guy?"

"It's me," I answered smugly. "Smart and good-looking. I didn't lie."

"Ugh. Just ugh." Katie muttered as she grabbed her apron off the hook. "How anticlimactic."

BY THE TIME I arrived back at my house with three coffees and one cappuccino, Ryan was already there and taking Tyler, his electrician, through the necessary wiring. When he finished talking with Tyler, he came over with his cappuccino.

"I think I might become addicted to these. Thank you, by the way."

"You're welcome. That's why I gave you the first two free, to get you hooked. Then you will keep coming back, and I will have a regular customer for life." I rubbed my hands together maniacally.

"I have a question for you."

"Fire away," I said.

"I have been speaking with a consultant about the possibility of expanding my business. He has been going over a few possibilities with me. But he said that the first step before we look too seriously at any particular option is to survey my current clients. So... would you consider being part of that survey?"

"What would that involve? A telephone questionnaire? Or filling out a form that you emailed me?"

"Well, I thought that to start with I would like to go

through the survey in person. Just so I can get a good feel for which questions I should add, subtract, or tweak. You aren't free Friday night, by any chance?"

My mind started swimming slightly. Am I free on Friday night? Like a date? No. This was about his business expansion. But why was Friday night sticking out in my brain? Oh, yeah! Sara had asked for the car.

"Yes. I am free Friday night. I won't have my car, though. Sara has already called dibs on it for her movie night with friends. So unless you wanted to meet here or somewhere close by, maybe another night would work better."

"That's great. Since you're free, and I'm free, and we both need to eat anyway... Why don't I pick you up here at six, and we can go over this questionnaire at a great Italian restaurant I like, about twenty minutes away from here? My treat?"

I was about to say no when my mouth just decided to do the talking without permission from my brain. "Yes, sure. Six o'clock will work for me," I heard myself say as I felt a growing panic.

"Sounds great," Ryan said as he gathered his things and headed for the stairs. "I will see you Friday at six. Looking forward to it." Then with a smile and no time to change my mind, he was gone.

THE REST of the week passed without too much excitement. That was a good thing because this date, er... dinner meeting with Ryan was almost constantly in the back of my mind. Why did I say yes? I still wasn't sure.

Friday morning came and, during a lull at work, I saw a text from my oldest friend in the world, Beth. Since I was on a break anyway, I decided to call rather than text her back. Beth answered on the first ring, and the background echo told me she was in the car.

"Hi Evie, so good to hear from you. It's been too long."

"What's this about you coming back to Haven from the big city? How long is your visit going to be?"

"It's not just a visit." Beth's voice sounded sad. "I don't know if you heard, but my dad is in the hospital."

"Oh no! What happened?"

"My dad had a heart attack—well, actually two heart attacks. Luckily, he was visiting with a friend when he had the first one, and his friend recognized the signs and called the ambulance. The doctors said that is the only reason he is still alive. Well, that and the fact that the second attack happened while he was at the hospital." I could hear the shuddering in her voice, and I knew she was holding back tears.

"I am so sorry to hear that. But I am glad he got to the hospital when he did."

"Me, too," Beth said, and I could hear the ticking of the turn signal going in her car. "Sorry, Evie, but I'm going to have to go. I have been running around like a chicken with my head cut off, trying to get everything sorted at work. So that I can use my vacation time to be there for Dad when he gets out of the hospital. The doctors say that even when he can go back home, he will need a lot of help with his day-to-day needs for a while. I have a meeting that I am just heading into to discuss the possibility of doing some of my work remotely, after my vacation days run out."

"Well, good luck with the meeting. And I will stop by to visit your dad in the hospital. Just let me know when you think he is up to visitors."

"Okay, will do, Evie. Bye."

"Bye, and Beth... take care of yourself. Let me know if there is anything that I can do."

"Thanks, Evie. Bye, talk soon."

That conversation left me feeling taken aback. Beth's Father, Gus Martin, had always been such a large and imposing figure. He had been a local football legend from Haven High back in the day. And he was such a friendly, down-to-earth kind of guy. He always called me "Other One" instead of Evie. Mr. Martin had begun saying that I was Beth's other half, and the nickname had just stuck. Beth and I had bonded back in grade three over our love for double-Dutch skipping and our hate for our grouchy teacher Mrs. Crabapple, as we called her. Her real name was Mrs. Crae. We have been the best of friends ever since. And even though her work as a ladies' fashion buyer for a large department store had taken her to the city, we still regularly made time to call or text. It was one of those friendships where, whenever we did get together, it was as if we had never been apart. I was sad about the reason Beth was coming back to Haven, but I was looking forward to being in the same town, even if it was just for a little while.

. . .

KATIE HAD AGREED to stay and lock up the café so I could get home and finish getting ready for this dinner meeting with Ryan. When she started getting the wrong idea about the reason behind this dinner, I made sure to set her straight.

"This isn't a dinner date, Katie. It's a dinner meeting to fill out a survey form he needs for his consultant. Nothing more," I said as I grabbed my purse and headed around the counter for the door.

"Well, that's a pity. Because the way he was looking at you when he was here, showing you his 'knobs'..." She made air quotes when she said that. "I think that he is attracted to you."

"You always think every man that comes in here is attracted to me. I hate to break it to you... but some men might be immune to my charms." With that, I headed out the door to my car, waiting in the parking lot for me. To overthink myself crazy... all the way home.

Chapter Five

After reapplying my lipstick, changing my blouse—nervous sweat—and changing my earrings four times, I was finally ready for my dinner meeting with Ryan. I don't know why I was feeling so nervous. When had I ever been this nervous over a meeting? I was being ridiculous; time to stop fussing and go out on the front porch to wait for him. Maybe swinging on the front porch would release some of this nervous energy.

Ryan arrived at the stroke of six o'clock, pulling into the driveway in his work pickup truck. In the time it took me to come down the porch steps, Ryan had already hopped out of his vehicle and was holding open the passenger door for me to get in. Passing by him so close, I couldn't help but notice that he had shaved since this morning, had on a fresh, white button-down shirt, and smelled amazing. Kind of like a fresh breeze with a hint of evergreen if I wasn't mistaken.

"Sorry about the work truck," Ryan said as he put out his hand to help my short little body up and into the cab of his truck. "I used to have a sedan, too, but being a single man, there wasn't the need to keep up with two vehicles."

I took his help getting in with as much grace as I could muster, although I suspect I must have looked like a three-year-old trying to climb up on the kitchen counter.

"I hope you like Italian food," Ryan said as he turned the key.

"What's not to like?" I smiled back at him.

"Any food allergies or intolerances that I should be aware of? I mean, if Italian food would be difficult for you to eat around, we could always go somewhere else."

"That's so nice of you to ask, but I can eat everything. Well, everything except for liver. And that's a choice, not an allergy."

Ryan laughed. "I hate liver, too."

"My mother always tried to get me to eat it by cooking it with bacon or fried onions, but it wasn't so much the taste. It was that powdery consistency on my tongue." I shuddered at the thought. "Oh, and I don't like kale. I mean, what's the point? It's so tough—just eat spinach and get it over with, without gagging on some woody stems. Do you want to hear a joke about kale?" I looked over at Ryan, busy driving and smiling away good-naturedly.

"Sure"

"Why does coconut oil make kale taste so good?"

"I don't know. Why does coconut oil make kale taste so good?"

"Because it makes the kale slide right off your plate and into the garbage can." I delivered the punchline with a flourish.

While Ryan chuckled at that, I gave myself a very stern talking-to about shutting the hell up! I mean, *kale* jokes? What was wrong with me? *Settle down, Evie!* It was silent in the car for a few moments until Ryan turned to me.

"Do you have a favourite radio station? Or a music preference?" He got a goofy smile on his face. "You like country music, don't you?" he asked before I had the chance to answer.

"Yes, yes, I do." I stuttered. "How did you know that?"

"From Archie's," he answered.

"From Archie's? The bar in town? I don't understand." I was busy trying to make sense of this; I was hardly what anyone would describe as a "barfly."

"Well, from karaoke night at Archie's, to be exact."

Oh no! My mind suddenly flooded with images of Katie and me getting our groove on at certain karaoke nights at Archie's.

"Please tell me I didn't make a fool of myself," I begged.

"Quite the opposite, in fact. You and Katie were up on stage doing a duet of a country song. I don't remember the name of it right now, but it will come to me. And before you ask, you and Katie really nailed it. I think that I prefer your rendition to the original. Katie was singing the man's part and had a surprisingly lower vocal range.

Sometimes, I think of it when I am feeling down, and it makes me smile."

I had now resorted to covering my eyes with my hands, like a small child who figures that if I can't see Ryan, he can't see me.

"How many times?" I asked, low and quiet.

"How many times what?" he answered, all innocent.

"How many times have you seen me sing at karaoke?"

"Just once." Then he added, "But that was enough."

"Ugh." Why, when you want a hole to appear and swallow you up suddenly, does it never happen?

"That night," he continued, "I just happened to be playing pool with some friends in the main part of the bar. I had just finished my game, and I heard singing coming from upstairs. I remembered that it was a karaoke night, so I took my beer upstairs to have a look. And there you were. Well, you and Katie. You girls were walking up on stage, and you looked... well... you looked like you both might have had a few shots of something for courage?"

Ugh. Just. So. Damn. Accurate.

"Well, I sat at a corner table and watched you two just slaying that song. When you finished, I remember the entire crowd stood up and cheered." His smile told me he was either really enjoying A) that memory, B) my discomfort, or C) both.

"I have a vague memory of that happening. Well... to be completely honest... a vague memory of that entire night. Katie and I were letting off some steam from a very long week, and we kind of... overindulged." That last part came out as a squeak, and my burning cheeks told me I was blushing. Ryan snuck a look at my face.

"I've embarrassed you—I'm sorry. I won't talk about it anymore except to say that you girls were very good. And from the ear-splitting cheering, I wasn't the only one that thought so."

Thankfully he then turned on the radio to a country station, and we rode along without the need to fill the silence anymore. I needed a few moments to gather myself. Katie—I blamed Katie! Although, from what I could remember, I think Ryan was right. I think we did slay that song!

As we passed the town sign for Bridgeport, where the restaurant was located, Ryan turned towards me again. "I think you're going to love this restaurant. Have you ever eaten at Naples' Son?"

"No. I have heard great things, though."

"I did a big renovation there a couple of years ago. That's how I met the owners and fell in love with their food."

"Well, I can't wait to see it. Is that why we're having this meeting there? To show me an example of your finished work?"

"I wish that I could say yes. That I planned to wow you into giving me great answers for my survey by showing you my completed renovations at Naples' Son. But I simply love the food." He waggled his eyebrows. "And the restaurant itself turned out amazing... if I do say so myself."

As we entered the restaurant, I could see that this was definitely not bragging on Ryan's part. The inside of Naples' Son was amazing. It had exposed brick walls, gorgeous wide-plank hardwood floors, and dark, moody blue walls. Usually, dark walls would make a place seem smaller or maybe feel more claustrophobic. In this case, though, the combination of the subtle layering of lighting from the sconces, pendants, and a candle in a votive burning on each table led to a very cozy and private atmosphere. In addition, the oversized stone and glass fireplace was placed in the dead center of the room. It was designed in such a way that the glass afforded everyone seated a great view of the roaring fire.

As Ryan was taking my coat, a man came running over and gave Ryan a big bear hug. The man appeared to be in his early sixties, with greying hair and a huge smile. He turned to me.

"Ryan, so good to see you. Your regular table is waiting, of course. And who is this beautiful young lady?"

I extended my hand. "Hello, I'm Evie. You have a gorgeous place here. And the food smells heavenly."

"Well," he answered, "the food, I will take credit for. The restaurant, however, looks amazing because of this talented fellow right here." He beamed at Ryan. "Did I tell you that my revenue is still increasing since the renovation? And that has been almost two years now."

Ryan patted his shoulder. "Yes, you tell me that every time I come in. And every time I come in, I tell you that, while my renovations might make some people come in for the first time, it's your food that keeps them coming back."

We were led to a cozy corner table and left with menus and the promise of a breadbasket coming right over. After Ryan ordered a club soda with lime, I ordered a glass of Italian wine, a Pinot Grigio that Diego, the owner, recommended. I began to feel a little more relaxed.

"You did a really great job on this place," I said. "What did it look like before the renovations?"

"You wouldn't have recognized it." Ryan shook his head. "The food was the same, amazing. But the atmosphere wasn't one you would want to linger in. The walls were all painted white, the floor was grey tile, and the lighting was all harsh pot lights. The artwork at the time..." He pointed up at the existing painting of a woman in profile, which I guessed was Italian in origin and softly illuminated from above. "It was all huge glossy posters of Italy. It kind of looked like a travel agency."

"Hard to imagine. Looking around now must be almost like looking at a totally different restaurant."

"Diego and his wife are hoping that their son Steve will take the restaurant over when they retired. They told me they wanted to leave him with the best start they could give him. That's where I came in. I think that this restaurant is my favourite project ever. I am very proud of how it turned out."

"As you should be," I said as I began to look over the menu.

. . .

THE FOOD WAS EXCELLENT, as promised, and the conversation was coming very easily. I had finished my meal and was contemplating dessert when I remembered the survey.

"We haven't started that survey yet."

"Yes, you're right." Ryan seemed surprised. "This evening has just seemed to fly by. Well, let's get started then." He pulled out a paper copy of his survey and began asking me questions about my happiness with his work so far. These questions began with Ryan's initial walk-through, then his men, materials, cleanliness, and everything in between.

Honestly, I didn't have any problems answering his questions because I was very impressed with all the work and planning that had gone into my basement. When Ryan got to the question of my satisfaction with the three levels of finishing offered, he suddenly stopped.

"I almost forgot," he said. "I wanted to ask you about the fireplace included in the second level of finishing. When I was taking Tyler through the wiring the other day, I pointed out the placement of the fireplace. That got me thinking about a fireplace option I think you will like, and I wanted to ask you about it."

"Okay, what options are available? Other than the one you included in the mock-up you showed me in the café?"

"Well, the option of that exact electric fireplace exists, of course. But I was thinking about your personal sense of decorating style. I noticed that you like to sprinkle antiques with your newer furniture. And that got me thinking about some antique Victorian fireplace inserts that I saw at an antique market in Bloomsberg. It's about a forty-five-minute drive from Haven. Have you ever been there yourself?"

"I have been through Bloomsberg, and I have heard of the antique market, but I have never been to it yet. Katie has been there with her husband, and she raves about it. We keep planning on going together, it just hasn't happened yet." I was surprised that he had taken so much notice of my decorating style—flattered, actually.

"If you're free next Saturday, I'm going to the market, and maybe you could come with me? That way, I could show you a few examples of this style of fireplace insert, and some antique mantels, to see if that is something you would like to explore?"

"I would really like that. I am free next Saturday, unless there is something that I am forgetting. You are right, by the way. I do love the look of antiques sprinkled with newer furnishings and artwork. And even though I am doing this renovation intending to sell my house, something feels right about finishing it in a way that is true to John's vision. It was actually John who had the eye for buying all our antiques."

Ryan smiled. "Saturday then, bright and early. It's best to be there when the market opens at eight. So I'll pick you up at your place at seven. My truck will come in handy if you decide to pull the trigger on anything there."

Saturday, I thought. It's a date. *No, it's not... It's just looking at options for the renovation project.*

Chapter Six

The drive home seemed much shorter than the drive there. But that's often the case when going anywhere. We filled in the ride back by getting to know each other a little.

I discovered that Ryan grew up on a working cattle farm just outside of Haven. His parents still lived on the farm, although Ryan said they were gradually taking on more help with the day-to-day running of the farm and that Ryan regularly lent a hand as well. He told me that he had two siblings—a sister Sandra and a brother Edward—and that he was the middle child.

He had been married to his first wife, Deb, for three years, separated for two years, and divorced for one.

I, in turn, told him that I had grown up here in Haven. That my grandparents had raised me after my parents died tragically in a car accident when I was six years old. I told him I had no siblings, but my best friend

Beth had undoubtedly filled that void. I shared that I married my husband, John, right out of university, and we were very happily married for twenty years. I teared up a little when I talked about John's cancer, and Ryan graciously offered me a Kleenex from a small pack he had in his glove box. I also told him that I was a proud graduate of Haven High.... Go Hawks! And it was at this point that I asked him which high school he had attended. Because, depending on where the farm was situated, he would either have gone to Haven High or the high school in a neighbouring town, whichever was deemed closer.

"Oh... Go hawks! Proud graduate of the Class of 2002!" he yelled, doing that wave hand-thing as best he could with one hand still on the wheel. "Funny thing about that," he said as he turned into my driveway. "I don't remember you at the school, and you, I think I would remember."

"It's no wonder we don't know each other from back then," I said. "I graduated Class of 1995."

Ryan was obviously quick in doing the math because, without even a moment's hesitation, he said, "Okay, so you are seven years older than me. That is quite surprising. I would have guessed you to be my age."

"Thanks for not saying 'You look great for your age!' I hate that saying! It's basically a kiss and a slap... you're well preserved, but you are still old."

Ryan looked surprised. "Age is kind of irrelevant once we are all adults. And your beauty doesn't grow weaker as you age. I don't think beauty ever grows old."

"That's a great way to look at it."

Ryan was already getting out of the truck, and I realized that he was coming to my side to help me down and out of the cab. "Thanks for coming with me tonight. I hate eating alone, and you were such a good sport about the survey," he said as he put out his hand.

"You're welcome. Thanks so much for supper, by the way. You know, you didn't have to pay for my meal."

"Cost of filling out a survey form: one meal with a beautiful woman. I think that I got the better side of that deal."

Once I was down and out of the truck, I stood very close to Ryan for a moment, and without thinking I just breathed him in. It had been a long time since I had been out anywhere with a man. Just over three years, to be exact. And I realized that I had missed it. Luckily, Ryan did not seem to notice me "sniffing" him.

"So, next Saturday," he said happily. "If I don't catch you before that here on the job. Remember, be ready for seven a.m. sharp. The best antiques wait for no man! Or woman!" With a mock tip of his hat, he was back in his truck and reversing down the driveway.

I waved back at him and then decided not to go into the house just yet. I could see from my car back in the driveway that Sara was home already. And I just wanted to savour the night in my mind for a little while longer before being bombarded by her teenage exuberance.

MONDAY MORNING I was trying out a new recipe that I just blindly put together. Even though raspberries were not yet in season, I had gotten a great deal on some at the grocery store, and I decided to include them in a brand-new type of scone. I would call them the Savoury Raspberry Scone, and they were a surprising and delicious combination of flavours. The raspberries would burst on your tongue with a hint of citrus, courtesy of some orange zest, and finished off with fresh basil that I'd snipped off my pot of basil, growing in the café's back kitchen window.

I was enjoying one myself, and by enjoying it, I mean cramming one down my throat as if I hadn't eaten in a week. When Katie walked in, she threw her gigantic purse on the clothes rack and almost toppled it over in the process.

"What's new, Evie?" She smiled and winked as she neatly caught the clothes rack before it fell to the floor completely.

"Savoury Raspberry Scones. Try one," I mumbled, my mouth still full of one of them. Katie grabbed a fresh scone off the cookie sheet, where they were cooling, spread some butter over half of it, and took a big bite.

"Yummy! It's another winner." She quickly devoured the other half too, this time adding some raspberry jam that I had in the fridge. "I think it's a tie between the jam and the butter." She winked. "Outside of food, what's new?"

"Well, today the electrician, Tyler, will officially begin the wiring in the basement," I said excitedly. "Oh, also, I found out last night that Beth's dad is up to visitors. I wanted to see if, sometime this afternoon, you could man the café by yourself for a while."

The front doorbell tinkled in the background, signalling the day's first customer.

"Sure, Evie. No problem. I'm just so glad to hear that he is starting to feel a little better. But when you get back from your visit, I wondered, when we have a few quiet moments... if we could talk about something."

"Yes, Katie. Of course." I was already running through disaster scenarios in my head about this "talk." Luckily, I didn't have much time to worry about that, though. The door was busily chiming away, and Katie needed my help.

LATER THAT AFTERNOON, as I entered the hospital. I felt a great sadness wash over me. The sights, sounds, and smells of the hospital seemed to be tainted by the remembrance of John's sickness and the amount of time I had spent here with him, so desperately ill. I found out from the receptionist that Mr. Martin was on the fourth floor, room 405, and the fact that visitor's hours were suspended at five o'clock for one hour to facilitate the patients' supper. It was only two o'clock, so I didn't anticipate that as a problem.

Mr. Martin, for such a large man, seemed somehow so small lying in that hospital bed. He awoke when I walked near the bed.

"Other One." He spoke softly and patted the edge of the bed beside him, urging me to come closer. "So good of you to come."

"Of course, I came. Just as soon as Beth told me you were up to visitors." I sat on the chair next to the head of the bed. "You are my only parent left," I said softly. I had always called Gus "my other Dad," and since my grandparents died, he was my last link to a parental figure.

"Beth and the doctors are just being overprotective. I could have handled visitors last week. But... they might have watched me sleeping a lot," he added sheepishly.

"Feeling a little better then?" I raised one eyebrow at him.

"Yes, much. Soon I will be able to go back home. With Beth's help and a steady diet of pills and appointments." He seemed resigned to this as his new reality. "Anything to get out of here."

"I was just talking to Beth last night. She said that she has her work schedule all figured out. Her boss gave her all her vacation days for this year and last, as well as negotiating some ability to work from home remotely after that."

"My Beth," he said with a sad smile. "I hate to be another burden on her shoulders."

"Stop that. You know Beth doesn't think about it that way at all," I admonished him.

"You know, she just seems so stressed all the time. Stressed and angry, not at me... of course... but still over all that nasty business with her ex."

I did know. I knew exactly what he was talking about. Beth had been through a nasty divorce just over two years ago. And while the marriage might be in the past tense, her anger certainly was not.

"Damn shame," Gus muttered. "That asshole really

messed with Beth's head, not to mention her wallet. I miss her laughter. She always had the best laugh. Right from her very first one, as a baby."

"It will come back," I said, with a lot more confidence than I actually felt.

Chapter Seven

Back at the café, Katie and I entered the afternoon lull, which usually happened around four o'clock. We had just finished wiping down and clearing the last of the tables when Katie turned to me.

"Do you have time for that talk now?"

Oh no! "The Talk"—how could I have forgotten to worry about that? It wasn't like me at all to waste an opportunity to overthink something.

"Sure," I said and sat down at one of the tables, pulling out a chair for Katie with my foot.

"I have started taking a night class at the local college." Katie began. "Hospitality Beverage Management, to be exact."

"Wow, Katie! That's great." But the wheels started to spin in my mind. What was she leading up to? Was she leaving me?

"I wanted to talk to you about taking on a bigger role here at the café."

"What would that look like?"

"I am hoping to expand my role as barista to include making a wider variety of beverages here, in-house." She looked over at me expectantly.

"What kinds of beverages were you hoping to serve? Not alcoholic, I suppose?"

"No, nothing like that. I understand that your café is just that... a café. Not a bar. But I think that we could serve so much more than coffee and tea beverages."

"Like?" I prompted her.

"Like bubble tea or Italian sodas? Or how about a Mexican Horchata? Or Strawberry Rice Milk? Also, I was thinking that I would like to start making in-house lemonade and iced tea in the warmer weather. But with a twist, like adding some savoury elements. Kind of like your Savoury Raspberry Scones from this morning. How about lavender or rosemary in lemonade? Or watermelon and basil iced tea?"

"Wow, Katie! You've put a lot of thought into this. But wouldn't I need to purchase some new equipment and a lot of new ingredients?"

"Yes, you would. That is why we could start small by adding in a couple of new drinks and doing a test run with them. If they don't sell, then we go back to just coffee and tea beverages. But... if they are popular, then we would slowly work up to making an even more varied selection of drinks and buying the new equipment and ingredients as we go."

"This would be a big change for the café. Can you give me a little time to think about it?"

"Sure, Evie. But . . . I also wanted to mention that I was hoping, if this idea of mine was successful, then along with my expanded role, I was hoping for a . . . raise?" She visibly cringed while saying that last bit. As if simply saying those words embarrassed her.

"Are you and Mark having money troubles? You know that you can come to me anytime. You don't have to prove your importance to me to get a raise when you need one."

Katie shook her head. "It's not like that at all. Please don't misunderstand. I know you see my importance here at the café, and I feel valued. Mark and I aren't having any money troubles. It's about... me, I guess. I want to do this. Take on this challenge and expand my role. If my ideas were to make the café more money, then getting a raise would be part of that."

"Let me think about it. If you could get me a list of additional equipment and ingredients that I'd need to have on hand? Then I will do some number crunching."

Katie started to get up from the table.

"Oh, and Katie? Congratulations on the college course. I am so proud of you!" I stood too and hugged her. "You are one of my best friends. You know me well enough to know that I don't adjust to change very quickly. Please don't take offence that I need some time to think about it. You have impressed me today with all your new ideas for the café."

Katie hugged me back. "Thanks, Evie. I'm proud of myself too."

It was then that Sandy appeared, right on schedule for the unsold baked goods.

"How has your day been, Sandy?" I asked as I walked back to grab the box of goodies from the kitchen.

"Good and bad. I mean, business is booming. But that's the problem—more and more families in Haven are relying on the food bank. To at least supplement the cost of groceries for their families. I don't mind the extra work, but it's just the reason behind it, and it kind of gets to me after a while."

"Losing the furniture factory in town was a tough blow to many families here in Haven. The new condo development on the site is great and all, but the new housing doesn't make up for the loss in jobs." I handed her the box.

"The condo development had nothing to do with the furniture factory closing. The nail went into that coffin a long time ago. Importing cheap furniture from overseas, and not enough people shopping locally, as far as I can see." Sandy said sadly. It was time to cheer things up a little, I decided.

"I was just about to invite Katie to come out for a glass of wine—on me. Why don't you come too? I think you've earned it." Sandy's face brightened and Katie said, "Yes!" at the same time, pulling a downward fist pump.

"Really? That would be great! Just tell me where to meet you girls, and I will be there as soon as I drop this back off at the food bank to be divided up into the food hampers."

. . .

AFTER A FEW GLASSES of wine with the girls and a brisk walk home, I was feeling good. Sara was still at her part-time job, so I decided to be lazy with supper and called for pizza delivery. If supper was going to be cold for Sara anyway, why not pizza? I sometimes even preferred it that way. After a phone call, my work for supper was essentially done. I headed back outside to grab the lawnmower out of the garage and try to get the lawn finished before the pizza arrived.

I CROSSED my fingers and silently prayed before pulling back the curtains. Yes! It wasn't raining, which meant my walk to the café where I had left my car overnight would at least be a dry one. Being Friday, everyone seemed to be in a good mood, and traffic was brisk in the café, which tended to make the day just fly by.

"Any plans for the weekend?" Katie asked.

"Yes. I am going tomorrow to that Antique Market in Bloomsberg."

"Oh? With who? We've been planning on going there together for what seems like a year."

"I know, and we will get there. But this is different. This is just a shopping trip for the renovations. It's for the basement, not for fun."

"Is Ryan taking you?" Katie smelled blood in the water. Abort, abort!

"Yes. But! He is simply picking me up in his truck, because if I find something I want to pounce on, I can. I mean, if I were to take my sedan, I could hardly bring a fireplace mantel back with me, now, could I?"

"Oh, so he *IS* picking you up. At your house?" Her smile was getting bigger and scarier, kind of like a Cheshire cat.

"Katie. When you're wrong, you are so wrong. This is a shopping trip and NOT a date. Whether he picks me up and takes me there or not."

"Whatever you say." Katie smiled sweetly this time.

"You're damn right it's whatever I say," I mumbled quietly to myself and walked away quickly.

LATER THAT NIGHT, I sat on the floor of my bedroom. Most of my clothes were strewn on the floor as well. Nothing seemed just right for antique shopping with Ryan. Why was I overthinking this? I told myself to just put on a pair of jeans and a black T-shirt. I was being ridiculous; I had skirts and dresses on the floor. What's next, I wondered... elbow-length gloves? How about a black T-shirt and a sweater just in case it gets cold? Oh, and a statement necklace? It was past eleven o'clock when I picked out a statement necklace and the perfect sweater. I piled all the clothes to one side of my room, went to bed, and set my alarm clock for early Saturday morning.

Chapter Eight

Ryan was amazingly prompt—I marvelled as he pulled into the driveway at precisely seven o'clock. I grabbed my sweater and purse off the porch swing and headed down the steps. Ryan met me at the passenger door. He was wearing a light blue flannel button-down shirt with a well-worn pair of jeans. His wet, slicked-back hair told me that he wasn't long out of the shower. The thought of him in the shower lingered a little longer in my head than I thought was proper. *Bad Evie! When would that thought be appropriate? Good thing that he can't read my mind!*

"Looks like it is going to be a great day, weather-wise." He beamed. "They said there was a thirty-percent chance of rain on the weather channel but look at that blue sky."

"Good thing," I said. I hadn't even thought about what to bring for inclement weather. Imagine how long that would have taken. I'm glad I didn't check—how would I have had the time for sleep?

This time the drive was much more comfortable. Chatting away with Ryan seemed to come easily, as did the occasional moments of silence to listen to a really good song that happened to come on the radio. And as promised, no more talk of that dreaded karaoke night. Although, when that aforementioned duet suddenly started playing on the country music station we were listening to, Ryan did get a massive smile on his face. For my part, I simply pretended not to notice. I did wonder to myself: had he requested the radio station play that song this morning? Surely not!

THE ANTIQUE MARKET WAS HUGE. I found myself lost in old framed art and small pieces of furniture like side tables and hall trees. Ryan was busy speaking to a few of his contacts in the antique salvage business. Architecturally interesting articles were saved by these people when an older house or building had to be demolished or during a renovation. Ryan would sometimes incorporate these vintage pieces into his renovation projects. On the way over, he had been telling me that the wide plank flooring in the Naples' Son project had been found at this market.

RYAN CAUGHT up to me later, wholly lost in antique kitchen wares. Original Pyrex dishes, coffee mills, kettles, bread boxes, and Ball mason jars. Especially the mason jars; I had already purchased six mason jars and a coffee mill when he caught up with me.

"I knew that you would love this place. You kind of get lost in the past here, don't you?"

I turned, surprised by his voice suddenly beside me, and I let him take my bags.

"Yes. So far I have found some things for the café. The mason jars are going to look so good holding loose-leaf tea, and that coffee mill will be a great antique for display." By now, I was walking through a section of vintage advertising, and a nice big poster for coffee caught my eye.

Ryan tapped my shoulder. "If you want, we can come back and I can help you. We can take our time going through these posters. A couple of them would look great on the back wall of your café. Behind the counter, if you don't mind me saying? Right now, though, we need to get over to the stall with the salvaged fixtures before we lose any of the newer fireplaces to some other buyer."

Ryan was right; I had simply fallen in love with the idea of incorporating an antique mantel and Victorian fireplace insert into the basement reno. Three hours later, my wallet was a lot lighter. Ryan had successfully managed to wrestle both the mantel and insert into the back of his pickup. I delicately placed my three vintage coffee and tea posters, rolled and secured with elastic bands, in a safe spot just behind my seat.

"Well, I don't know about you, but I'm starving." Ryan turned to me in the truck.

"I could eat," I said, but words weren't really necessary, as my stomach, grumbling loudly, seemed to be speaking for me.

"There is a BBQ restaurant just up the road. They claim to have the 'World's Best!' BBQ ribs. And after you taste them, you won't be claiming false advertising."

"Lead on, good sir." I joked and silently thanked the powers that be that I had worn a black T-shirt. I was notorious for slopping sauces... well... food in general, on my front shelf. My large bosom seemed destined to be a catch-all for food and drinks, much to my embarrassment.

THE RESTAURANT WAS, as advertised, simply the best BBQ I have ever eaten. I ordered the ribs against my better judgment for slopping potential, not to mention face smearing. And in the end, when I checked myself in the bathroom mirror, I found no sauce on my face and only one small spot of sauce on my shelf. Luckily—because of my black T-shirt and the fact that I had picked a molasses-based sauce—it was very hard to see.

When I arrived back at the table, I found that Ryan had ordered us both coffees and a piece of pineapple meringue pie to share. I had never tried a meringue pie in any flavour other than lemon. But it turned out that Ryan was right: it was delicious. The shared eating of it had a surprisingly intimate feeling. I hadn't shared a dessert since John. And even then, I had to be very full to agree to share! I mean, this is dessert. Hello!

Ryan wouldn't hear of me paying the bill or even my

half of the bill. He said that it was his idea to go out for lunch. But let's face it, my loudly grumbling stomach was likely to blame. When I went to set some bills on the table for the tip, Ryan stilled my hand.

"Instead of you leaving a tip, let me look after it. Because I have a favour to ask of you."

I looked expectantly at him, wondering what favour he would need from me.

"Can you play pool?"

"Can I play pool? Yes, John and I played sometimes. Despite that, I'm still not great at it. I mean, I know how to play. But if you are looking to win? Then you are looking at the wrong girl."

"Are you free next Friday night?"

"Yes, but... don't you think you should ask someone else? I am not that skilled a player."

"Great. Next Friday night, eight o'clock at Archie's. I will pick you up at quarter to eight."

"Are you listening to me? You. Will. Lose."

"I am most definitely listening to you. You will do just fine. This is a friendly game that me and three of my good friends play on the last Friday of every month. My usual partner, Tom, has broken his arm in a motorcycle accident, and I need someone to sub in for him."

"Yes, but... your friends don't know me. You should pick someone else."

"No, you will fit right in. My friends are very welcoming to 'strangers.'" He mimed air quotes. "And I am pretty sure they don't bite." He lifted his top lip to bare his teeth.

"Okay, I guess. You don't need to pick me up, though. I can meet you at eight o'clock in Archie's."

"No, I will pick you up. That way, you can have a couple of drinks if you want to, and I can drive you home."

"What if you want to have a few drinks too?"

"Well, as I see it, if we both end up drinking, then it will only be my car left in the parking lot when we Uber ourselves back home. Sound good?"

I was trying to find a flaw in his logic, but I couldn't. "Sounds good."

Ryan just smiled and slid out of the booth to grab my sweater off the hook nearby and hold it out for me to put on.

WHEN WE ARRIVED BACK at my place, Ryan helped me get the mason jars, mill, and posters in my house. He said he would get help from one of his men to get the mantel and fireplace out of his truck and into the storage area of his shop.

"I'll stop by on Monday to speak with Tyler and discuss the wiring with him. I'll make sure he doesn't have any questions and tell him about the fireplace, confirm the location, and go over the dimensions. I think you made a perfect choice today. That fireplace insert with that mantel... well, it's going to be a showstopper when we are finished." He then turned to go down the steps and suddenly stopped and turned back around. "Oh, and don't forget about Friday night. It's just a fun game, and you will like my friends. Looking forward to it."

He was in his truck before I even had the chance to argue or second-guess my decision. I guess I am going to play pool with Ryan and his friends next Friday. Heaven help me!

Chapter Nine

Monday morning was crazy busy. Then, suddenly, it was a ghost town. I asked Katie if she would mind making me a vanilla latte; I wanted to have a shot of caffeine and put my aching feet up for a few stolen moments. Katie agreed and made me my latte and herself a cappuccino. She brought them over and sat down across from me with a sigh.

"Monday," she groaned. "Am I right?" We toasted each other with our coffee mugs. "I am so glad we finally have a quiet moment to talk. I have been dying to find out how your date with Ryan, the hunky contractor, went." She then proceeded to stare at me across the table with her head resting in her hands.

"You are just trying to wind me up, and it's not going to work. It was just a shopping trip."

"For the renovations..." Katie finished my sentence for me. "Blah, blah, blah. Get to the juicy parts. Did he hold your hand? Carry all your shopping for you? Take you out for lunch?"

How does she figure this stuff out? I did the best that I could to deflect. "Hold my hand? No, don't be ridiculous. Now, let me go and get us each a muffin." I said to throw her off the scent.

"Okay, so what you are saying, or actually not saying, is that he *did* carry your shopping. AND... he *did* take you out for lunch after. Don't forget to warm mine and add a pat of butter." Damn it, she was good!

"Listen, he only carried my shopping because it was heavy. I mean... I bought six mason jars AND a coffee mill. That's just being polite. I am a small woman, after all. And as far as lunch goes, he only took me to the restaurant because my rumbling stomach would have distracted his driving." I laughed a little, remembering it. "It was almost deafening."

"I am hearing a big hunky man comes to your rescue and takes you out on a lunch date. One more question before I retire to my chambers to deliberate and come to my verdict. Did he pay for your meal?"

My voice cracked as I said, "Yes," then I banged my head softly on the counter.

"Guilty... of being on a date." Katie could be insufferable at times.

LATER IN THE WEEK, Beth called me to tell me that she would be arriving next week. Her dad was to be discharged on Tuesday morning, and she had made all the final arrangements with work in order to come to

Haven and look after him. I invited her to come to my house for supper just as soon as she had her dad all settled in at home. I couldn't wait for a good catch-up with Beth; talking in person was just so much better than texts or phone calls. Also, it was sure to include some big-girl glasses of white wine and a chocolate dessert.

Sara and I were getting ready on Thursday night to go to a question-and-answer meeting for students applying to college or university and their parents. We decided to walk there, as the night was one of those warm spring nights without a cloud in the sky. Sara was excitedly telling me about the girls she knew who had also applied to some of the same three universities she had. I was surprised to learn that her best friend Olivia had also applied to the University of British Columbia for the Environmental Sciences program.

"Well, good thing you know other friends that have applied to the local universities," I said. "That way, no matter where you go, you won't be alone."

"It will be okay no matter where I go, Mom. I mean, I will definitely be making new friends, no matter what. Because I don't know anyone else that has applied specifically for the Psychology program."

"Also, if you get in locally, that means that not everything will be new. You will be able to live at home in the town that you grew up in and sleep in your own bed. And no concerns over student residence life distracting you or lousy cafeteria food."

Sara just nodded in agreement. She suddenly

grabbed my hand to hold while we walked. Something she hadn't done since she was a little girl. We walked along in silence for a while, and then she squeezed my hand.

"I know that you worry about me, Mom. But I want you to know that no matter where I go or how far away... I am going to be just fine. You raised me to stand on my own two feet. And we will always find a way to talk regularly, whether texting, zooming, or phoning."

"Or, if you get in locally... fighting over the bathroom in the morning."

"It's really not a fair fight, Mom, not when I always win."

At that point, I realized we were just around the corner from The Penthouses. The building was beginning to rise out of its concrete foundation, and the sight made me feel a little buzzing of excitement in my stomach. There was a new sticker added to the billboard that said "Phase One - Sales Centre Now Open."

Sara stood in front of the chain-link fence, looking in at the construction site. "Do you think you'll have to buy your condo soon? It looks like they are starting to sell them, even in the pre-construction phase."

"With the renovations underway at our house, I don't want to put it up for sale yet. The whole idea of the renovations was to try and get a wider range of potential buyers from the in-law suite, not turn them away because my basement is under construction. Don't worry," I told Sara. "In a town the size of Haven, The Penthouses is hardly going to sell out any time soon."

"I'm sure you're right, Mom. Now pick up the pace, we are going to be late."

FRIDAY MORNING CAME, and I was silently congratulating myself over not stewing about the game of pool tonight with Ryan and his friends. My congratulations were short-lived, though, because I was almost dizzy with nerves by the afternoon. Although I was wary of speaking about it with Katie, I finally reached my breaking point. You know the saying... any port in a storm.

"Katie, I am a little worried about tonight at Archie's."

Katie looked surprised. "Did we plan to go to karaoke and I forgot?"

"No, Ryan asked me to sub in at a friendly pool game tonight."

"Another date, huh?"

"No, I just happen to know how to play pool, and Ryan's partner broke his arm."

Katie gave me a stern look. "I want you to know that I could bug you right now about this being a date. But... you look so nervous that I will let that go. Now, what has got you so worked up?"

"It's not the 'pool' side of things. I know how to play. Not well, mind you, but I know how to play. Also, Ryan insists that it is not a competitive game."

"So, what's the problem then?" Katie looked genuinely concerned.

"It's Ryan's friends," I said. "I don't think I'll fit in. I don't think that we will have anything in common."

"Why do you think that? Do you know these people?"

"No, it's not that. It's just that Ryan is seven years younger than me. And these are old friends of his, so they will probably be around the same age as him."

"Why would that matter so much?"

"Seven years... is a long time. It can make a difference between people being in totally different stages in life."

"Like?"

"Like, none of them will have an eighteen-year-old just about to start university. They will most likely have kids in grade school, or maybe even babies."

"So... you think that if these people have young kids, then you will have nothing to talk about?"

"Yeah, I just don't want to stick out as different, I guess."

"You are overthinking this, Evie. Remember that you're telling your troubles to a mother of three young kids, and somehow, I still find you interesting."

"Thanks, Katie, you're right. I am blowing this all out of proportion, aren't I?"

Katie nodded her head. "Now, let's talk about something that really matters. Like, what are you going to wear?"

Chapter Ten

After a shower, curling my hair, and three sets of clothing changes, I finally decided on an outfit. I chose a pair of comfortable and flattering black Ponte pants with a slightly distressed vintage No Doubt T-shirt. I topped them with a jean jacket and some cute ankle boots with low heels. I decided that the overall look was young—without looking like I was trying too hard to *look* young—and had a definite casual feel. Just right for a night at Archie's. I decided to have a glass of wine out on the front porch to help calm my nerves. As I set the empty glass on the railing, Ryan pulled into the driveway.

"You look great, by the way," Ryan said as he helped me into the truck.

"Thanks. I will admit to you that I feel a little intimidated."

"Why, because you haven't played in a while? I can give you a quick refresher when we get there."

"No, not about the game. Although, I am not being modest when I tell you that my skills aren't great. It's more about playing with your friends; I think I will be the odd woman out."

"My friends are... well, friendly. That sounds... never mind, my friends are always welcoming to new people. So you can relax. It's going to be a fun night. Tom will be there too, by the way. Not to critique your game, just to hang out with all of us. He said that his one working arm could still hold a beer. You'll like Tom. He's my oldest friend, and he is laid-back and funny... like you."

"He sounds great," I said as I put my seatbelt on. "But as funny as me? I doubt it. No one is as funny as me." I suddenly realized I was feeling a little less nervous after talking it over with Ryan. "Thanks," I added softly.

Ryan reached across the seat and squeezed my hand. "Any time."

ARCHIE'S WAS busy and kind of loud when we got there. His friends arrived just after us, and they had to yell a little to be heard over the music. Tom introduced himself first and thanked me for subbing in for him tonight. He explained that he had a fluke accident on his motorcycle; I didn't catch absolutely everything he said, but it had something to do with turning a corner and an unexpected puddle. Next to arrive was Chad, followed almost immediately by Lena. I found out Chad was a friend from college, as was Lena, although apparently, Lena had been in a different program.

It was a relief when we were able to move to the back

corner of the bar, where the pool tables are located. It was a lot quieter back there, and finally we could speak without yelling. Tom generously offered to get the first round of drinks.

As Lena and Chad were giving him their drink orders, Ryan leaned in to ask something quietly in my ear. "Are you okay with me having a few beers tonight? I know that means we would have to Uber home. You know, though, if you have to get up early tomorrow, I could just have a club soda or something. It's up to you. Anyway, I had thought that since it is such a nice night, maybe we could walk?"

"I have no problem with that and nothing to get me out of bed early tomorrow. I think it's a nice night for a walk. That's why I wore my low heels, just in case I felt like walking home."

"Well, that's settled then. What is your usual drink of choice?"

"White wine, usually a Pinot Grigio when I am at home. But at Archie's, I always order a frozen lime margarita. They do them up so perfectly here. Just the right mix of salty and sweet. I like to ask for extra salt on the rim, because some of it always falls back into the drink... yummy."

At this point, I realized that Tom had been waiting for our orders. Ryan asked him for a particular craft beer that I had never heard of, something with a funny name like "Beer There, Drank That," I think. Then he ordered my frozen margarita; he even remembered to ask for the extra salt on the rim.

After Tom put in our order for drinks with the

waitress, we headed over to their regular pool table and began to play. Ryan and I won the break, and we ended up choosing stripes, with Lena and Chad left with solids. The game was going quite well, and I was surprised to find that I was holding my own. Ryan was right; his friends were very welcoming. They would occasionally talk about things from the past or inside jokes that I had no idea about. However, they were always careful to ask me a question afterwards and include me in the conversation.

It turned out that Chad was happily married with two kids—one boy and one girl, aged ten and six.

Tom was divorced with one child, a girl, who at seven was going back and forth between his ex's house and his own. One week on and one week off. He said that it wasn't perfect, but the fact that they both lived in town meant that it worked for the most part.

Lena was single and had been out of a long-term relationship for about a year now. She had no children and said that she was focused on her career right now.

When the questions turned to me, both Chad and Tom spoke glowingly of my café, and both of them said they had been in, mainly on Saturday mornings. They seemed surprised that they'd never met me there. I explained that my two university students were long-time employees and that they ran the café quite efficiently on Saturdays in my absence. Lena said that she had never been to my café. In her defence, she didn't live in Haven; she lived in the neighbouring town of Northport.

I explained that I was a widow and mother to Sara. I

spoke a little about her excitement about applying to university for Psychology. No one made any mention of Sara's age or seemed surprised by any of my answers to their questions, and slowly I began to relax more and more into the evening and their friendship.

About halfway through the game, I started to notice that Lena was always watching Ryan, sneaking furtive glances when she thought he wasn't looking. All at once, she turned and caught my eye after she realized I had asked her a question while she was seemingly lost in thought, gazing at Ryan.

"Sorry, I didn't catch that," she said, a glaze of red creeping up her neck to her face.

"I just asked, what it is that you do for a living?"

"Oh, I'm an architectural technologist. Chad, Ryan, and I all attended the same college. With those two"—she pointed at Ryan and Chad, currently smack-talking each other over the game—"in the Construction Management program. Architectural Technology isn't traditionally a career loaded with other women. But I love it. Currently, I'm working for an engineering firm. I am hoping, though, shortly, to start my private practice by providing building design services to the public."

"That's exciting. Owning your own business is rewarding."

After that exchange, Lena seemed to be a little more careful to try not to be caught watching Ryan. I did still see her catching small glances, though, when she thought she wouldn't be noticed.

All in all, I found my nerves were unfounded, and I was surprised when the game seemed to have flown by and suddenly all the glasses were empty. One by one, Ryan's friends said their good-byes, ribbed us about our loss, and headed home. After a few moments of looking for my jean jacket, I turned to find that Ryan had been holding it out behind me to help me put it on.

"Thanks," I said. My jean jacket on and my purse in hand, we walked out the door and into the night.

I OFFERED to walk myself home after I found out that we lived on opposite sides of town. Nevertheless, Ryan insisted on walking me home. He said he wouldn't feel right about letting me walk home alone in the dark. We decided to walk to my house, and he would order an Uber back to his house from there.

We had been walking for a while, talking mainly about the game that night, with Ryan reassuring me that the loss tonight was not unusual. Being pretty evenly matched, he said, both sides seemed to win and lose about half the time. I had been thinking about Lena and how she was sneaking glances at Ryan all night.

"You should ask Lena out on a date. I noticed her watching you all night. I think she has a crush."

Ryan stilled suddenly. "What?"

"Well... I mean, it's pretty clear to see... maybe as a woman... that Lena seems to be... interested in you." I know I'm babbling now, but I just can't seem to stop. "And you're single... and she's single... and you obviously like each other..."

"As friends," Ryan replied curtly. All of a sudden, I realized that while I had continued walking down the street, Ryan had stopped walking and was staring quite intently at me.

"What's the matter? I'm sorry if I overstepped. I mean, I don't really know you... or her..."

"Why?" Ryan asked. "Why would you ever think that I would ask another woman out on a date when I am on a date with you? Do you think that... that... that's the kind of man I am?"

Whoa! What did he just say? A *date*?

"I didn't realize this was a date." I stammered. "I mean, you just needed a substitute for your pool game."

"Did you think that? That... I asked you tonight only because I couldn't find anyone else?"

"Well... yes. I did. I mean, we don't really know each other. And I am so much older than you..."

"I told you before that age is just a number once you reach adulthood. And I meant that." He grabbed my hand and started walking again. "And... dating is how people get to know each other."

We walked on in silence for a few moments, my mind trying to make sense of all of this. I could see my house just ahead. As we walked up the driveway, Ryan stopped, but he didn't let go of my hand. Instead, he squeezed it gently. "I have a confession to make," he said, looking into my eyes.

"What is it?" I mean, was there more?

"I am attracted to you. I've been attracted to you since that night I saw you singing karaoke at Archie's." He took a big breath. "And... the first two dates, well, I know that you didn't look at them as dates. But I want to be clear, from now on, that I want to get to know you better. And..." he continued, "I am aware from speaking about you with my sister Sandra that you typically . . . don't date."

Sandra? Sandy! Sandy from the food bank was his sister? Did they talk about me? About my feelings about dating?

Ryan squeezed my hand again. "I can see your mind spinning at a million miles an hour. Sandra has mentioned you a few times in the past—all good things, by the way. She talked about you in such glowing terms. Anyway, when you spoke to her about your basement renovations, she asked me if I was the one doing your renovations. Long story short, I told her that I was thinking of asking you out. And... she told me that she had overheard you say that you don't date. So I decided to spend a little more time with you than was strictly necessary... to try and get to know you. To see, if once you got to know me... if... maybe, you would change your mind about dating. Me, I mean."

I was too stunned to speak, move, or think.

"I hope that you don't think any less of me. Just to be clear, I want to be very up-front about my intentions from now on. I want to date you, properly date you. And I know that I have probably shocked you. So I want to give you some time to think about this. Next Friday night, I would love it if you would join me for dinner and a movie. If you are interested, just let me know by text or call me or... in person. If we happen to see each other here." He gestured at the house. "I am interested in you, and I hope you feel the same way about me. But if you don't... It's fine. No hard feelings. We will just maintain our usual business relationship. Or we could just be friends. Whatever you want. For what it's worth, thanks for tonight. I really enjoyed it."

"Oh... you're welcome." I managed to mumble.

Ryan fumbled for his phone from his pocket and pushed the app for Uber. "Good night," he said, turning his attention to his phone.

"Good night," I mumbled. Then I somehow got myself in the house and up the stairs and checked on Sara, who was fast asleep. I was still reeling from Ryan's revelations when I fell into bed.

Chapter Eleven

The following day I would have typically treated myself to a lazy lie-in. In this case, though, my swirling thoughts would not allow that to happen. Had I missed all the signs? I am older than Ryan, but did that mean that we shouldn't date? Did he eventually want kids? And with me over that stage in my life... how would that work? Did I even want to start dating? These thoughts kept me busy as I started my weekly cleaning routine. Sara woke a couple of hours later and stumbled noisily down the stairs for a cup of coffee.

"You're up early," she said sleepily as she made her way over to the toaster with a slice of bread. "You usually love to sleep in on Saturday mornings."

"I just woke up early and then couldn't get back to sleep—you know how that goes." Sara nodded as she pushed the lever on the toaster.

"How was last night, by the way? You were helping out a friend by playing pool?"

"It was fun. I haven't played in so long, I thought I might be rusty. But I think that I did okay. Even though we lost. I mean, I did warn him that I wasn't very good."

"You haven't played pool since before Dad died. I am glad you went out. Did you see Katie at karaoke by any chance?"

"No, Katie was having a much-deserved date night with her hubby."

"Ugh. Hubby, that word is so lame. What's wrong with saying husband, or you know... Mark, his actual name?"

"Hubba, Hubba, hubby. I just like the sound of it." I waggled my eyebrows at her and smiled. Sara knew when to bow out, and she grabbed her toast and headed back upstairs to get ready for her shift at the drug store.

THE REST of the day I found my thoughts constantly circling back to the question of officially dating Ryan. I wasn't going to kid myself. I knew that I found him more than a little attractive. Yet the idea of officially dating filled me with a sense of unease. So many questions came to mind. I like Ryan, but the thought of dating him was making me feel... guilty? Did that mean that I wasn't ready to date? I still had days when I struggled with my grief. Was that fair to Ryan? What would Sara think? Would she think that I was moving on or letting go of the memory of her dad? I decided that maybe it was time for a quiet talk with Sara. Maybe at Sunday dinner tomorrow. I could make her favourites, and we could talk about her dad, about the idea of me dating, and about her feelings. Making sure she knows that how she feels about this is important to me.

That decision was made. And I felt a little lighter somehow. I then continued with my weekend household cleaning routine to the beat of my music playlist. As I was bopping around, dusting and sweeping, I realized something. The music I was cleaning to was the same music I used to party to. *Wow,* I thought, *when did I become this old?*

SUNDAY TURNED out to be dark and rainy, a perfect day for cooking. Sara went to Olivia's in the afternoon to work on a science project they had to do together. She had promised me to be home for supper by six. I was hustling and sweating over the stove all afternoon. The finished dinner included all of Sara's favourite dishes, complete with White Chocolate Macadamia Nut Cake for dessert. Which is quite a large cake for two people. At the end of the day, though, I knew I could always pawn any leftovers off on Katie and her brood.

Sara sat down to supper and instantly became suspicious. "What's wrong?"

"Why would something have to be wrong?"

"You made all my favourites, and it isn't my birthday. So that means something is wrong, or you have big news that I probably won't like. Or both."

Well, her momma didn't raise no fool! "Nothing is

wrong," I said with an uneasy smile. "I just want to talk to you about something."

"Oh, here we go. I knew it. My spidey senses were tingling." She wiggled her fingers in the air.

"First of all, I wanted to check in with you. I know that you are still meeting with your online teen grief support group. I wanted to know how that's going and how you are feeling."

"I look forward to those meetings. I find that having those other kids that have gone through the same kind of loss and sadness... is almost like having an instant group of supportive friends. Friends that I can try out an idea or some feelings on, that sometimes just pop into my head. Because they know exactly what I am feeling or going through."

"I'm glad to hear that you are still getting so much out of your group." I reached across the table and squeezed her hand. "I still meet with my support group too, but not as often anymore. I check in with them from time to time. Especially when I am feeling overwhelmed or just so exhausted."

"I still keep finding parts of my life that feel like bits are missing from. Dad-shaped bits. Like when I sent out my applications for university. I had this strong urge to tell him, and that was hard, but I just had to hold on to the knowledge that Dad would have been so proud of me."

"So very proud." I blinked back the unshed tears that had begun to fill my eyes. "You are so young. You will have so many firsts that you will wish you could share with your dad. But knowing him the way only a daughter can means that you will always carry him with you."

"It's always going to hurt, isn't it? Sometimes I feel it sitting like an elephant on my chest, and other times it's farther away, and I'm just waving to it from a distance, like on a safari or something." Sara looked around for something to scoop up the pasta with and found nothing, so she quickly walked into the kitchen, grabbed a large fork and spoon from the drawer, and brought it back to the table. "But I have the feeling that there is maybe something new going on with you. You seem to be a little more... tied in knots this weekend? And ALL my favourites... at one meal? I'm starting to feel like maybe I'm on death row." She smiled cheekily at me from over the table, where she was now eagerly filling her plate with her beloved Garlicky Shrimp Pasta and Bacon Citrus Spinach Salad.

"Death row? Teenagers are so dramatic. Nothing as bad as that, I can assure you." Although maybe someone should tell my stomach that, because the idea of eating pasta and salad was beginning to feel like a hill too high to climb. "I have met a man," I said as I mentally steeled myself to continue this sentence, "and I am thinking about possibly dating him." There—it was out of my mouth, at last.

"Who is this man?" Sara asked. I was closely watching her face for any reaction of hurt. Or sadness or anger? Seeing none of these reactions, I continued.

"Ryan, his name is Ryan, and you have met him here at the house. He is the contractor that I hired to finish the basement."

"That makes sense." She smiled at me as she wiped some creamy sauce off the front of her blouse where it had landed on her shelf. Like mother, like daughter, I thought.

"What do you mean... it makes sense?"

"I have only met him a couple of times, but I have noticed how he looks at you."

"You have?" I was genuinely stunned.

"More importantly... I have seen how you are with him."

"How am I with him?"

"Lighter, a little more... full of life somehow. You get this look on your face as if you have something happening that you're excited about, or maybe... just really looking forward to something. And... it has been too long since I saw that look on your face."

"So, you think that you could be okay with my dating again? Do you think that I am being disloyal... or embarrassing? I mean, even just the idea of dating again is huge. I thought that dating was something I would never have to go through again. I had your dad. I had the love of my life. I don't know if I can even open myself up to someone new. How will another man understand me or understand what I have been through? Something that I am still going through."

Sara didn't say anything for a moment. Then she slowly stood up and walked around to my chair. She crouched beside me and took my hands into her own.

"You are a lot of things, Mom. But disloyal? Never. Embarrassing... sometimes. I mean, like when you turn up the volume of one of your old pop songs just so that all the kids will turn and look at me when you drop me off at school? Yes, sure. But the idea of you dating again? No." She looked up to meet my gaze. "You asked me what I thought about the idea of you dating again. And now I am going to tell you exactly how I feel about it. Happy. I mean... with a touch of concern for you, but generally happy. You deserve to have some fun. And from my support group, I know that there is no kind of guidebook for this type of thing... you know... like instructions on how to handle these types of feelings, or... how to do this correctly."

She stood up from her crouched position and grabbed my empty plate to take to the sink. "But if he hurts you... I might not know people, but I'm sure that I must know people that know people. And..." She then drew her finger across her neck. "It'll be curtains for him." She said it like she was a 1930s gangster.

And with that over in her mind, like a typical teenager, she was already on to the next thing. "Cake time!" She announced loudly and proceeded to cut us each a big piece.

Chapter Twelve

Katie was happily working away at making her first in-house Lavender Lemonade and Watermelon-Basil Iced Tea. I had agreed to test the appeal of these two new drinks, with spring here and summer around the corner. In part because the cost of adding these two drinks to the menu was minimal. The other beverages that Katie wanted to add included more expensive ingredients and equipment. I still hadn't been able to get a complete idea of the total cost. So, Katie and I agreed, for now, to start with the two cold drinks to test the market.

I had just finished adding the two new drinks to our blackboard when Katie appeared at my side. "Oh my gosh, in all my excitement over the new drinks, I forgot to ask how playing pool with Ryan and his friends went."

"Well, you were right. I was worrying too much about it."

"And no one even thought twice about your age, did they?"

"If they did, they hid it well. I had a lot of fun, and the evening went by fast."

"Are you planning on going out with Ryan again? I know you said it wasn't a date, but I think that you two look good together."

"You have been trying to tell me that I would 'look good together' with every handsome single man that has come through these doors in the last year. So excuse me if I don't take your word on the matter as a ringing endorsement."

"I would be lying if I said that was untrue. But you know that I care about you and your happiness. I pride myself on being your biggest cheerleader."

"Oh, that reminds me—I was thinking of instigating a café uniform. Maybe a short skirt, a sweater with a big 'E' on it, and pom-poms?"

Katie laughed at that. "Can you imagine? The lineup would be around the block." She then proceeded to mime spelling out Evie with her imaginary pom-poms.

"In all seriousness, though, Ryan did ask me out on a date. For this Friday night, dinner and a movie." I then proceeded to tell Katie about Ryan's admission and my subsequent talk with Sara.

"So, what was your answer?" Katie asked, suddenly serious. I never got to answer that question because Ryan walked in at that very moment.

"Hi, Evie," he said with a big smile, then he turned. "Hi, Katie. You should be aware that your boss here has a real criminal mind."

Katie smiled back. "Oh, that so?" She quickly turned and pretended to need a cup behind me on the counter so she could whisper just loud enough for me to hear, "Let me guess... she stole your heart?"

I love Katie like a sister, but also like a sister, I would love to strangle her occasionally.

"Yes, she set out with trickery and manipulation to make me addicted to your cappuccinos."

Katie laughed at that. "Oh, that. She does that all the time." Katie began to tamp down the espresso grounds.

Ryan turned to me. "So that is five dollars?" He took a five-dollar bill out of his pocket and handed it to me. I pushed his money back at him across the counter.

"Your money is no good here. Not as long as you are finishing my basement."

"But you're paying me to renovate your basement. So how does that work?"

"It works because I say it works. Now put your money away. How about a muffin to go with that cappuccino? Can I tempt you into trying one of my Lemonade Muffins?"

"And get me addicted to muffins as well? I don't think so." He had a smug look on his face, and he was busily jamming the bill back into his pocket.

"Suit yourself. They just came warm out of the oven, and they are a mix of tart and sweet with a sugar-crusted top. I recommend having it with a pat of butter. Oh, and a cappuccino, of course." I echoed his smug smile.

Ryan patted his flat stomach. "How am I to keep my weight in check with you tempting me with delicious-sounding baked goods all the time?"

"You poor dear."

Katie slid his cappuccino over to him, and I noticed that in the foam, Katie had artfully made a heart with an arrow through it. Subtle, Katie! Real subtle. Ryan grabbed his oversized cup and saucer.

"If you can spare a few minutes, Evie, I just wondered if you could make a final decision on the style of lighting that you want for the kitchen. Tyler is at your house today, and he called and said that he thinks he will be able to finish the kitchen wiring today. So, pot lights? Pendants? One long rectangular pendant over the island, and pot lights? I have some examples of the lighting choices with me on my laptop."

"Sure, I will be right over. Wow, Tyler is good. I didn't realize that he would be finishing the kitchen already."

UNDER KATIE'S WATCHFUL EYE, I pored over the lighting choices with Ryan. In the end, I decided to go with a mixture of two sconces on either side of the kitchen window, pot lights on a dimmer over the sink, and a long, rectangular pendant that would hang above the island for a more focused working light. I was happy with the choices that I made. Brass antique replica sconces, modern flush pot lights, and a feature pendant that was at the same time modern and traditional, with its sleek lines and inset crystals dangling.

When we finished with the lighting choices, Ryan kept his word about not pressuring me. He thanked me for the coffee and headed back over to the house to give

Tyler the specifics of the dimensions and locations of the wiring needed for my lighting choices.

AFTER THAT, though, there was nowhere to hide from Katie's question. What was my answer going to be? I was pretty sure I was going to say yes, but I still wanted a few more days to exhaust all possible outcomes in my mind. When I told Katie that—not in those exact words—she surprised me.

"I think that's smart, Evie. Don't let yourself feel rushed into making this decision. Take your time, and make sure that it's what you want." She then proceeded to pour both of us a Lavender Lemonade topped with a cute sprig of lavender and a slice of lemon hanging off the side of the ice-cold glass. We clinked glasses, and I must admit that it was delicious.

Chapter Thirteen

Tuesday afternoon came, and I managed to get home a little early to start supper. Today was the day Beth was officially back in Haven. She had called after she got her dad home and settled. She told me that he had insisted she come out to visit with me tonight. Of course, that was after she had made him a simple supper, adhering to the hospital dietitian's rules. She told me that her dad had his meal waiting for him to heat up in the microwave, and with no more medication required for the day and his phone beside him on the bed, she was free for the rest of the night. That meant she felt confident she could come by tonight for dinner and a catch-up.

BETH ARRIVED about twenty minutes late, so by Beth's standards, that meant right on time. She dropped her bags on the floor and gave me a big bear hug.

"I missed you so much," she said into my hair and then stepped back to look at me. "You are looking great, as always. My fashion sense has clearly rubbed off on you."

"Oh, stop it." I gently slapped her arm.

"I bring presents." She proceeded to rustle through the bags and produce a large bottle of white wine, an Italian Pinot Grigio, and a box of French chocolates. Only the best would do if Beth were bringing gifts.

As we settled into the kitchen, Beth perched on a bar stool at the kitchen island while I was still putting the finishing touches on supper.

"So your holiday time officially starts today?"

"Yes, I get four weeks total—two from this year and two unused weeks from the year before. I haven't taken any holidays for a few years now. They might have been a little too happy to give me this time off." She laughed in a hollow sort of way.

"Well then, their loss is definitely our gain."

"It smells so good in here. What are you making for supper?"

"My famous Spinach and Artichoke Tortellini Pasta, with a salad for health purposes. And... extra cheesy garlic bread, in case of vampires."

"Always thinking ahead, that's my Evie. But seriously, who would want to be a vampire? Live forever? Yikes. Some days, I just barely make it through as it is." She smiled at this as if she was making a big joke, but I could see some of the truth in what she was saying shining through.

Beth was looking around, swivelling on the bar stool. "I forgot how big your house is." She swivelled back to look at me. "So... what's new with you? I feel like it's been forever since we had a proper catch-up." Beth began nibbling on a small charcuterie board I had whipped up earlier.

I filled her in on Sara and her university applications, and I touched on the renovations I'd started in the basement and how it would be a stand-alone one-bedroom apartment upon finishing.

"Wow, you have been busy. But why are you finishing the basement when you already said that the house is too big for you and Sara? Especially with Sara about to head off for university?" I was struggling to get the cork out of the wine bottle.

"Well... I am renovating the basement in hope of getting a better price and more competition when I sell. As far as Sara leaving home, two of the three universities she applied to are at Haven's doorstep. She will still be living with me for a few years."

"Speaking of Sara... where is she? I was hoping to see her too."

"I'm afraid you will need to stop by another time for that. She has volleyball practice tonight, and then the girls usually go out for pizza."

"Okay, make sure to tell her that I said hi. Getting back to the house... selling? Where are you thinking of moving to?"

"Did you happen to pass the lot on First Street that

used to have the old furniture company on it before it was knocked down?"

"Yes," Beth said. "I saw a sign about some sort of condo project coming soon."

"They just recently broke ground on it. It's called The Penthouses, and it's going to be very high-end. With ten-foot ceilings and large balconies, and you know... all the finer finishes that you would expect." I paused to take a breath. "All that, and I can walk to the café in a couple of minutes. Just think how much easier it will be for me when I don't have this huge house to clean. Or the grass to cut, or the snow to shovel?"

"That sounds great, Evie. I don't want to rain on your parade, but you know... I miss my house, sitting in the backyard on a patio chair, puttering in the garden. You might end up missing your yard. Even if that means you have to mow it."

"The house is just a little too big for Sara and me." I looked up at Beth through the rising steam of the pasta I was draining in the sink.

"Oh, I don't know about that. You might miss all this space if you were stuck living in a broom closet, like me." She gestured wildly around the room with her half-full wine glass.

Beth had moved into a small two-bedroom condo in Toronto two years ago after selling and splitting the money from her three-bedroom house in a lovely little up and coming neighbourhood. The house was situated in a coveted location, within walking distance of cafés, restaurants, and shops. The move was made necessary by her snake of a husband, Chris. Who, unbeknownst to

Beth, had been having a year-long affair with her good friend and next-door neighbour Candice.

Beth had loved that old house and fixing it up through the years had been a labour of love. Her love of all things fashion did not end at ladies' wear, and she had proven herself to be exceptionally talented at home renovations and interior decorating. So, in the end, the house she loved was sold. Beth moved into a high-rise condominium about a mile and a half away from the neighbourhood she had become so devoted to. Chris, on the other hand, had taken his half of the money and slid over next door into Candice's house. Which meant that not only was Chris still able to live in a similar style house in Beth's beloved neighbourhood, but Chris's half of the money was now spent on lavish vacations for himself and 'Candy.'

"Bon appetit," I said as we sat down for supper.

"Speaking of houses..." Beth hissed. Oh no! I realized too late that this was a dangerous subject to be getting into with Beth. Ever since her divorce and losing her house, her good friend, and the love of her life all in one fell swoop, she tended to fixate on the subject. I set the finished pasta on the table.

"You will never believe what Chris and Candy did to their front yard."

"What did they do?" *Ugh! Help me, someone? Anyone?*

"They had two giant cement lions on tall pedestals placed on either side of their driveway. Have you ever heard of anything more egotistical in your life? I mean...

okay, maybe in front of a mansion? But in front of a three-bedroom house? Ridiculous!"

Beth's voice was gradually getting louder and angrier. As if merely thinking about those lions made her want to punch something. Or someone? Someones? Is that even a word... someones?

"How do you even know about that? I asked. "Your new place is so far away from there. I doubt that any of your regular chores or work are taking you out there just by accident." I was careful to look inside my wineglass when I said this so as not to have to make eye contact.

"I drove by. I wanted to see if the new owners of my house had changed any of the front landscaping." Beth had worked tirelessly on transforming the front lawn into a beautiful perennial garden. Without any help from Chris, as usual.

"I thought that we agreed you weren't going to do that anymore. I don't think continually going by the house is helpful. I know that it's hard to move forward. Never mind moving forward while looking in the rearview mirror."

Beth didn't even try to look contrite. "I know what I said. But Evie... seriously. They ripped my garden out. I mean, they pulled out every last plant. I saw them, all yellow and dying, in a large dumpster in the driveway. And do you know what they replaced it with? Grass!" With that, she accidentally dropped her fork on the table, and it clattered to the floor. "Sorry about that." She bent down, picked up the fork, and began wiping it with her napkin.

"You know that I have more than two forks. I can get

you a new one." I put out my hand to replace the utensil.

"No, no, no... It's fine." Beth made eye contact with me across the table. "He wins, you know," she said, quieter now. "He wins, and she wins. Did you know that they just got back from a safari in Africa? Do you remember... my bucket list trip? The one that Chris and I were going to take to celebrate when we... when I... finished with the renovations?" She dropped her head into her hands, defeated.

"How do you...?"

"Facebook. I still follow Candy under a false account that I set up."

"You know that I love you, right?" I asked as I went around the table to hug her. She nodded through her tears. "But you have to stop this. It's holding you back. It's been two years now. I don't want to watch you short-change yourself. You have too much to give."

The rest of the meal passed without any more tears or outbursts from Beth.

"I'm sorry, Evie. So sorry; I don't know why I am always going on about them. Especially with you, after all that you've been through."

"Everyone has their bad times, Beth. It isn't a competition."

As I waved good-bye to Beth from the front porch, I couldn't help but miss the old Beth. The sweet, quick-to-laugh friend who was filled with self-confidence and seemingly never-ending energy. Her high school nickname had been "Energizer."

I realized that even though I had just spent the evening with my best friend, I still missed her.

Chapter Fourteen

The basement was changing in front of my eyes. This morning, when I returned to talk with David and Paul, I was surprised to see that not only was the framing and electrical wiring now complete, but they were currently hauling drywall sheets into the basement. I was thinking about how much different the basement would look once there were actual walls when David and Paul came down the basement steps, and I handed them their coffees.

Paul, as always, made sure to over-thank me for the coffee. "You know, you are our favourite customer. Have I told you that already?"

"Many times, Paul. But it's always nice to hear."

David took his first long sip of coffee, probably his first of the day, and sighed audibly. "He isn't just saying that to you, you know. You really are the current favourite client."

"Current, huh? What do you think I need to do to cement this position?"

David looked over at Paul. "Cookies?"

Paul silently shook his head, so David corrected himself. "Muffins?... Bagels, maybe?" When Paul nodded, David repeated. "Bagels." And without any further consultation with Paul, he added. "With cream cheese. But really... Paul does seem to really like working with you. And so do I... I mean, you are involved without being too involved, if you know what I mean. You bring us a coffee every day, and that's nice and all, don't get me wrong. But more than that, you are interested in our job, and you make sure to be available every morning to answer any questions that we have. Not everybody does that, you know."

Paul seemed a little embarrassed at this surprising confession from David, and he was busily slurping his coffee and looking vaguely around the room.

"Thanks for that, you guys. I appreciate the work that you're putting into my basement. My husband, John, would be so excited to see the walls coming up." Secretly, I had been hoping I would see Ryan at the house this morning. "Is Ryan expected to be in today?"

Paul grabbed his phone and checked for any new texts from Ryan. "It looks like he won't be here today. He has been called out to another job. What can I do for you?"

"Oh, nothing. I will just talk to him later, that's fine."

"I can probably answer your question, though. In Ryan's absence, I am in charge. So how can I help you?"

"That's nice, Paul, except in this particular case... I don't think that you can help me."

"Is this maybe a question that is a little more personal in nature?" Paul asked, and he and David exchanged knowing glances.

"It just isn't a question about the renovations... exactly." Yikes, this was beginning to get awkward. "I will just text him, maybe."

"Do you have Ryan's personal number to contact him? You know, like outside of his work phone?" Another small but perceivable glance was shared between them.

"Yes," I said with as much nonchalance as I could muster. Then I made a speedy exit back up the stairs before they could ask me any more questions.

INSTEAD OF GOING STRAIGHT BACK to the café, I drove to a particularly pretty park and pulled into a parking spot. If I was going to call Ryan, I didn't want to do it from the café, where I might be overheard. I didn't want to leave the call until tonight, either. So, I took a deep breath and dialled the phone.

Ryan answered on the third ring. "Hello." It was obviously very noisy where he was because the commotion in the background made it difficult to hear him.

"Hi, Ryan. It's Evie calling."

"Oh, Evie. So good to hear from you."

Maybe this wasn't a good idea; he was obviously busy right now. "Maybe I should call you another time. It's kind of noisy, and I'm having trouble hearing you."

"No, just give me a minute, and I will go outside and get away from all this construction noise."

True to his word, after a couple of minutes of background noise, it was suddenly just Ryan that I could hear.

"Evie, can you hear me good now?"

"Yes, that's better. Listen, I am calling because... well, because... I have had some time to think about officially dating, and I have come to a decision."

"Okay."

"I tried dating about a year ago. Katie did some matchmaking with a man her husband was friends with. I had been convinced that it was something that I should try. So, I went on one date, just one. And... it was a disaster. Luckily, I hadn't talked to anyone about it ahead of time—other than Katie, of course. It was horrible and really embarrassing. And it was after that terrible date that I made my 'not dating' rule."

Ryan was very quiet on the other end of the phone.

"Anyway, I have taken a few days to think about this and talk it over with Sara. Long story short, I have decided that you are nothing like that other man. And after getting to know you a little... I realized that I want to get to know you even better. I think that maybe I am ready to try this again. Only this time, it will be because I really want to. Not because a well-meaning friend thought that it would be good for me."

Ryan's voice filled the phone again. "Phew! I thought your answer was going to go the other way for a minute. So, Friday night? Dinner and a movie? Do you have any preferences? I mean, I think that you should pick the restaurant. After all, I picked Naples' Son and the BBQ place."

"What do you think of Thai food?"

"I love Thai food. The hotter, the better."

"Why don't we pick the movie when we get to the movie plex after dinner? Kind of just go with whatever is showing next at that time. I mean, I'm not picky... unless you are?"

"Sounds great, Evie. I am not picky about what kind of movies I see. I will see just about anything. Except for musicals. I have to draw the line somewhere." Then he added. "Do you think that you would feel comfortable talking about that date? About what went wrong? I just want to be sure not to do anything that might trigger or upset you."

"Sure, I don't see why not. It's a little embarrassing... but sure. Well, to begin with, this gentleman was a friend of Katie's husband, Mark. And I use the term gentleman loosely, very loosely in Hugh's case. Mark's friend Hugh had met me in the café, and I guess he asked Katie if I was available because he was thinking of asking me out. Katie was so excited by that idea that she started a kind of campaign to make it happen. After a few weeks of that, I agreed to go on a date with him. That way, if it was a good experience, I could decide if I wanted to move forward with dating him. But, if it were terrible, I would, at the very least, get Katie off my back."

"Sounds like you were pushed into something that you just weren't ready for."

"It was more than that. To start with, he booked us a table at Archie's. I thought, not exactly a nice restaurant, but it was a familiar place, and that made me feel comfortable. When I arrived, he was polite and seemed to feel quite confident, which would normally be a good quality. But Hugh was overconfident. I mean, he seemed to think that he was 'all that and a bag of chips.' He talked only about himself—bragging, really. He never asked me any questions about myself. He just didn't seem interested in getting to know me at all. He seemed so sure that, of course, I would... I don't know... maybe just be so happy to be out with him? I think he thought himself a much better catch than me, maybe because I am a widow? I'm not sure. Then, to top that horrible night off, he announced that while he was attracted to me, he wanted to be clear that he was only interested in being friends with benefits rather than dating."

"What a jerk! What did you say to that?"

"I said, 'Let me get this straight. You don't want to be friends, and you don't want to date me. So you just want to have sex?' He seemed surprised by that."

"I just bet." Ryan mused.

"I said, 'Hell no!' Actually, I didn't say it—I yelled it. People started staring. Then he had the gall to ask me, 'Why not? I'm attractive, you're attractive, there is nothing wrong with just having a little fun.'"

"With a widow that lost her husband of twenty years?!" Ryan seemed angry on my behalf.

"So, I told him, 'Because I have more respect for myself than you apparently have for me.' Then I grabbed my purse, threw a twenty-dollar bill on the table, and called him a wanker on my way out the door. Truthfully, I yelled that too."

It was silent for a second, and then Ryan's laughter filled the phone. "Wanker? Where did that come from?"

"I watch a lot of British murder mysteries. I guess some of the slang has rubbed off on me."

"Perfect, just so perfect." Ryan took a deep breath and seemed to be struggling to stop laughing. "Thanks for sharing, Evie. You have nothing to fear about a repeat of that experience. I can't wait for Friday night! Can I pick you up at seven? Will you make a reservation? Or do you want me to?"

"I will, and Ryan? Thanks for listening. I am looking forward to Friday too."

Chapter Fifteen

I found myself running behind on Friday morning. Apparently I had woken to my alarm, shut it off, and then gone back to sleep. I had planned on curling my hair and spending extra time on my makeup. Now, however, I'll be lucky to manage to get the baking finished before the morning rush starts. Luckily, I had carefully set my outfit for the day over the chair in my bedroom the night before. After pulling on my clothes and putting my hair into a ponytail, I ran out the door. It wasn't until Katie pointed it out that I realized I had put my top on inside out.

"You're really kind of nervous about tonight, aren't you?" she asked. "You poor thing, all tied in knots. This doesn't have anything to do with your experience with Hugh, does it? I still feel responsible for that fiasco."

"I am not 'tied in knots' about tonight. The opposite, actually. I had a really great night's sleep. So good, in fact, that I shut my alarm clock off this morning and then went back to sleep. Besides, why are you still feeling responsible for Hugh? That's just not fair to you. Hugh made the experience bad all by himself. Without any help from you."

"I pushed you into it. I had the best of intentions, in my defence. But I should have given you the room to decide when you felt ready to get back out in the dating world. I'm sorry about that, Evie."

"Katie, let it go. I have. And never doubt that I always view your actions towards me as being motivated by only the best of intentions."

"Thanks, Evie. Now tell me, where are you going to eat on your date tonight? Actually—more importantly, what are you going to wear?"

"I chose that Thai restaurant. You know, the one that just opened last month?"

My mouth was watering at just the thought of some chicken pad Thai and spring rolls for a side. Oh—I hope they serve fried bananas. So delicious! Coated with sesame seeds, coconut flakes, and deep fried, I loved them served with coconut ice cream. The hot bananas would start melting the ice cream, and the resulting crunchy, creamy, sticky mess was a treat I loved to scoop up by the spoonful. That is an excellent idea for a new muffin. What about a banana muffin topped with coconut-flavoured whipped icing decoratively piped on top, and the finishing touch would be a piece of fried banana stuck in the top of the icing? And I would call it "Evie's Gone Bananas."

Lost in delicious thoughts of fried bananas, I wasn't

listening to Katie, and it was becoming evident that she had asked me something.

"Sorry, Katie, can you repeat that?"

"I was just saying that you should choose either a romantic movie or a horror. Either one should work."

"I am pretty sure I shouldn't ask this, but I am going to. Why would my two movie choices only include a romance or a horror? No, better yet—what do either of those two movie choices have in common with each other?"

" A romance will get him in the mood for, well... romance. And the horror will scare the bejesus out of you, and then he will comfort you. And comforting you will lead to touching, and touching you will lead to..."

I cut her off at this point, as she was, likely, heading into a tangent of some sort on physical intimacy with Ryan.

"Thanks, Katie. I think I got the picture. You're very helpful."

Katie winked at me. "Now for your outfit."

We debated whether a dress was too dressy or if jeans were too casual, and then on to my hair: was it better up or down? Finally, my outfit settled, I was just about to return to the kitchen and start inventory when the café door opened, and Trouble walked in.

And by Trouble, I mean a very good-looking, tall without being lanky, very self-assured man. We had nicknamed him Trouble because he seemed to be a master of flirting and flattering any woman's pants off. And I mean that literally. Katie and I had been witness to Trouble...

well, working diligently on turning the head of any and every good-looking woman he came across. I don't think he deliberately went looking for women who were already attached, but I did know of at least one married woman who, after being hounded by Trouble, was very quickly divorced. The worst part of that story was the fact that, after a couple of weeks of dating Trouble, he dumped her via text and then was on to the next sweet thing. Now Trouble knew better than to go after Katie. Trouble had run into her husband, Mark, and apparently Mark had made it quite clear that flirting with his wife was essentially flirting with danger. Trouble might be devious and a complete hound dog, but he was not stupid. Trouble's smile widened when he saw me walking back to the kitchen.

"Hey, where are you going, Princess?"

I nervously adjusted my ponytail. "Hi Sam, I have some inventory work that I have to finish. Katie can look after your order, though. Nice to see you." I was now doing a speedy walk—well, as quick as these high heels I had decided to wear today would allow me to go.

"I was hoping for an audience with the Princess. It will only take a moment. Please?"

I backed up, but only a few steps. "Yes, Sam, what can I do for you?"

His wolfish grin told me that my phrasing was not the best. "What can you do for me, indeed? You are taking me to places in my mind, Evie."

Silence, just silence. I knew better than to try to engage with him when he was in full hunting mode.

"Evie, I am trying to keep away from dairy. It just

isn't agreeing with me lately. And anyway, I haven't seen any dairy alternatives listed on your blackboard?"

He looked almost uncomfortable at this point. Inside I could feel a smile desperate to sneak out of my face at the thought of Trouble all flatulent from the dairy in his daily latte. That would definitely make all the ladies give him a big swerve. The smile was beginning to become quite painful to hold inside.

"Of course, Sam. Katie can make your regular latte with either soy milk or almond, whichever you prefer." I snuck a quick look at Katie to find her trying to cover her laughter with a coughing fit.

"Sure thing, Sam." Cough, cough. "Coming right up. Which would you prefer, almond or soy?" Katie managed to squeak out.

I took advantage of this exchange to make it as quickly as my heels would allow back to the kitchen and away from Trouble. As I turned into the kitchen doorway, I overheard Trouble saying something to Katie about how good I had been looking lately. Ugh! That man—no matter how many times I politely said no to him, he just kept coming back. I didn't want to be rude to a customer, but with Trouble, it was getting hard not to be.

BACK IN THE kitchen after my inventory was finished, I found myself thinking about tonight. I was still a little conflicted about the idea of dating again. I knew that I wasn't going on this date to stave off loneliness; I had long since come to terms with my own company, my hobbies, and my friends and family to fill that void. Nevertheless, I could admit to myself that I had begun to miss physical and emotional intimacy. I missed being kissed good-bye in the morning and warm, comforting bear hugs after a bad day. I missed the way John's warm leg somehow found mine every night in bed. But I wanted to take things slow, make sure I didn't rush into anything, and risk heartbreak on either side. I was worried that maybe I would find myself comparing Ryan to John. After twenty years with someone who knew me better than any other person on earth, dating someone new would take some getting used to.

Katie agreed to lock up tonight, as my nerves were getting to me, and I was basically useless by late afternoon.

I HEADED HOME early and managed to arrive at precisely the same time that Sara got home from school. After asking how her day had been, I reminded Sara about my date tonight. She just smiled and told me to have fun. Apparently, she had made plans with Ann tonight. They were going bowling, and then she said she was going to Ann's house to sleep over. I made sure that I had Ann's phone number and address, just in case of an emergency. After I gave Sara permission to wear my new designer coat, she cheekily thanked me, and that was when I saw it peeking out of the unzipped backpack on her shoulder. I guess asking for permission after taking it was better than never asking at all.

· · ·

By the time six-thirty rolled around, I was putting the finishing touches on my Katie-approved outfit. Dark jeans with a bright red blouse, set off with a long necklace that had a large yellow crystal dangling. Large gold hoops, and it was all topped off with the cutest pair of yellow ankle boots you have ever seen. I always felt more in control when I was dressed to impress, even if I only impressed myself.

This time I didn't make it out to the porch to wait for Ryan because he rang the doorbell a full fifteen minutes early.

Chapter Sixteen

"Hello, Evie. You look amazing. And I love that necklace you have on," Ryan said as he stepped inside the house. "Sorry about being so early. I've actually been sitting in your driveway since six-thirty. I knew I was here way too early, but I guess I was feeling a little excited about our first official date tonight."

Ryan stood in the front foyer with his keys in one hand and a small, colourful bouquet of flowers in the other. I was taken aback by the sight of him. He was wearing a crisp, blue button-down shirt with some slim-fit khakis. His regular work boots were gone, and a pair of freshly polished brown Oxfords were in their place. When I stepped forward to accept the flowers and take them into the kitchen to find a vase, he leaned forward and kissed my cheek softly.

"Thank you so much for these," I said as I stopped to

smell the bouquet. "It's been a long time since I was given flowers. That was very thoughtful of you."

"You're welcome. I thought about bringing you a box of chocolates too, but that seemed cliché."

"You can never go wrong bringing chocolates into this house!" I yelled at him from the kitchen. The flowers were now safely arranged in a vintage milk bottle and I headed back to the foyer.

Ryan smiled at me. "Good to know. I will hold on to that knowledge for the future."

"Well, it's not a 'get out of jail free' card... but it might just grant you bail." Ryan grabbed the sweater sitting on the front bench and held it open for me to put on.

THE THAI RESTAURANT smelled wonderful and the atmosphere was carefully cultivated. There was a small rectangular pool in the center of the restaurant with a statue standing at one end and floating on the crystal-clear water there were various flowers and herbs. The seating had an intimate feeling, and the lighting was a series of gold-painted, round wicker pendants.

The host put out his hand to pull my chair out for me, but Ryan beat him to it. Once seated and our drink orders taken, we gazed at each other over our menus as we marvelled at the vast array of choices. I ordered my usual chicken pad Thai, and Ryan decided on the green Thai shrimp curry. We agreed to share my favourite spring rolls, and Ryan also talked me into trying the golden purses. Fried wontons closed like a drawstring purse with the help of a chive, filled with crab meat and spiced with cilantro, garlic, and some hot chili pepper. They ended up becoming a new favourite of mine.

Ryan started talking about the renovation work in my basement. He was quite pleased with the way the work was progressing. I told him how happy I was with Paul and David's work.

"They are big fans of yours, as well," Ryan said.

"I know—Paul and David told me that. It's nice to hear again, though. I mean, who doesn't want a fan club?"

"I don't know if you know this, but I've joined your fan club as well. We meet every Wednesday night and are thinking of having T-shirts made."

"Oh, please tell me they'll have a big picture of my face on them." I laughed.

The meal continued with great food and easy conversation. Since Ryan had already heard my terrible date story, I asked him to share his worst date ever.

"I hadn't dated for nine months following my divorce. I just didn't feel ready. Too busy licking my wounds, I guess. Well, a couple of my friends got together. You met one of them at billiards, Tom? Tom and Ben decided I just needed a little nudge. So unbeknownst to me, they had set up a profile for me on a dating website, and they surprised me with a date. They told me I was really going to like this girl they had picked and that she was just my type. I don't know why I went through with it, but they were really pushy about it, so I said I would meet her for one dinner date. The date started off well enough—we talked about our jobs and our families. She seemed bright and outgoing, and she was rather pretty. By the end of dinner, I thought that this had actually been a good idea. I was feeling better than I had in months. I asked her if she wanted to continue the date with a nightcap at Archie's. She said that she was having a lot of fun and agreed that we would both drive our cars over and meet there. But as soon as we got outside, I knew something was wrong. She kept saying 'NO, no, no' and looking around the parking lot wildly. When I asked her what was wrong, she said that someone had stolen her car. I immediately phoned the police to report a stolen vehicle. Then, suddenly, a furious man pulled up alongside us, rolled down the window, and began to scream that he was going to kill me. It turned out that the woman I was on a date with was married, and she had been fighting with her husband. She had phoned him when she went to the toilet during dinner, rubbed it in his face that she was on a date, and told him which restaurant we were at as well. That was the first and last date that I have been on since . . . well, since you. Tom and Ben felt bad about that fiasco and immediately took down my dating profile."

I had to admit that was one of the worst dating stories that I had ever heard.

"So this is why you always like to drive?" I joked.

"Well, let's just say that I'm not taking any chances."

THE MOVIE we ended up choosing was a comedy; it seemed like a safe bet. Unfortunately, the laughter was canned, and the jokes were just vulgar, without being at all funny. I found myself not paying any attention to the movie after a while, and instead I found myself staring at Ryan.

I enjoyed just taking him in for a while. His attention was on the screen. His beard was well trimmed, and he had a few laughter lines around his eyes that crinkled when he smiled. His nose was long and straight—not too big or too small. And sitting this close to him, I couldn't help but fixate on the warmth of his shoulder and thigh where they touched mine. He smelled fantastic too, and I was just letting my mind go to a place where I wondered what his lips would taste like when he turned and caught me staring. He smiled at me, and silently he crept his arm over my seat and around my shoulders and gently squeezed. I lay my head on his shoulder and nestled into his warmth.

The rest of the movie passed in a blur, and if asked under oath to describe what had happened in the film, I couldn't tell you, because the warm flush on my cheeks and the racing of my heart was taking up all my attention.

When the movie ended and we left the theatre, Ryan held my hand as we walked to his truck. As Ryan usually did, he walked with me over to the passenger side and opened the door. Instead of just putting his arm out to help me in, he turned and gently wrapped his arms around me. He tilted his head and looked down at me for just a moment, and then he softly kissed me. My heart started hammering away until it was all that I could hear. Then, as suddenly as it had happened, it was over. Ryan pulled back from the kiss and wordlessly put his arm out to help me into my seat.

The ride home from the movies was not a long one, and we listened to the radio without talking. I was still lost in that kiss and the butterflies it had released into my stomach.

WHEN RYAN PULLED the truck into my driveway, for just a second I panicked that the house was completely dark. Where was Sara? But then I remembered she was going to her friend Ann's house after bowling. Ryan shut the truck off.

"Thank you so much for such a wonderful night, Evie," he said softly. But the look that he was giving me was turning my mind to jelly.

"You're welcome," I managed to respond before my body just took over. I leaned over to grab his face in the palms of my hands and kissed him. Not a quaint romantic peck, but a full-on passionate kiss. I wanted to satisfy my earlier musings and find out precisely what he would taste like. And apparently it took quite a while for my brain to decide that I now knew *precisely* what he tasted like. Time seemed to stand still. Ryan's hands cradled the back of my head, holding me at just the right angle to kiss me. He then pulled me forward and kissed the top of my head. He sighed softly into my hair.

"Evie. What you do to me . . ."

Suddenly the atmosphere just seemed too serious.

"So, no jealous boyfriend wants to kill you at the end of our date. Does this mean it was a success?" I asked, to lighten the mood. But Ryan's face was still flushed, and his gaze was soft and deep.

"This date was most definitely a success," he answered softly. The look on his face made me want to grab his face again and kiss him, slowly and deeply. But my brain told me that the smartest thing to do was say good night.

"When can we do this again?" he asked as he helped me down from the truck.

"What were you thinking?"

"I was thinking that next Friday night I should show off my cooking skills on the grill and have you over for supper." Ryan had reached out and was twisting a tendril of my hair around his finger lazily.

"That sounds amazing. What time should I arrive? Oh, and more importantly, I don't know where you live."

"I will text you my address, and I think that, if you want, you could come by a little earlier than dinner—let's say five o'clock. That way, you can have a glass of wine and keep me company while I barbecue."

With that sorted, we said our good-byes, and when I fell into my bed, sleep came quickly, with the memories of the night still fresh and playing in a loop in my mind.

Chapter Seventeen

Sara and I had a lazy Sunday morning together, including making ourselves a big breakfast. After digesting, we began to divide up the dusting and vacuuming. It always made the housework seem more manageable when we used a divide-and-conquer approach. To reward ourselves for a job well done, I made us a big bowl of popcorn, and we laid around on the couch for the rest of the day watching Sara's favourite horror movies.

"Mom, put your hand down from over your eyes, it's not that bad."

"No way. I can tell from the ominous music that the killer is just waiting to strike."

When the last movie ended, we started talking and catching up on the week. Sara told me that Olivia had broken up with her boyfriend of three weeks and that she was heartbroken. She spoke about her job at the drugstore and that she had talked with her manager about the possibility of getting full-time hours this summer to start putting more money away for university expenses. She said that school was going well and that her guidance counselor had told her that she could possibly see letters back on acceptance from the universities within a few weeks. She seemed almost giddy with excitement at the possibility of opening an acceptance letter so soon.

And I wanted so badly to be able to talk to John about it all. About how proud and happy I was for her, but also about my sadness at the idea of her eventually leaving the nest.

She also asked me about my date on Friday night. I told her that we had a great dinner and that the movie we picked was a dud, but that all in all I had a really good time. Then she asked me if I was considering going out with Ryan again. I told her truthfully that I really liked Ryan and that we had already made plans for the weekend. She seemed genuinely happy to hear that and even asked me a few questions about him. It felt awkward talking with my daughter about another man, a man that wasn't her father. But Sara seemed to take it all in stride the way only a teenager can.

"Okay, Mom, sounds good. Now I have to go and video chat with Olivia." With that, she vanished upstairs to her bedroom, leaving me alone with my thoughts. Thoughts of all the changes to come in our lives and the vague sense of unease that it left in my stomach.

. . .

A COUPLE OF DAYS LATER, when Sandy arrived at the café for her usual collection of day-olds, I could tell from her body language that something was up.

"Is everything okay, Sandy?" I asked.

"I just wanted to make sure that you knew I wasn't gossiping about you."

"What do you mean? Why would I think that?"

"I was talking with Ryan on the weekend at Mom and Dad's, and Ryan happened to mention that he told you about me having been the one to tell him about your 'no dating' policy. And I wanted to make sure that you didn't get the wrong idea. You know, like, maybe you think I go all around town talking about your personal business."

"Oh, I never thought that."

Sandy visibly relaxed. "Well, thank goodness for that. I would never go around talking about you behind your back. It was just that Ryan and I got talking. And then your name came up, and he told me he was thinking of asking you out. I just didn't want him to feel bad when you said no, or for you to feel uncomfortable saying no because he is finishing your basement."

"Sandy, I think of you as a friend, and I wasn't upset about it. It wasn't exactly a secret that I had a strict 'no dating' policy."

Sandy looked kind of embarrassed. "Is it true, though? Are you and my brother officially dating?"

"Well, yes. I mean, it's early days yet... but, yes."

"I am so glad. You are so sweet, and Ryan is so kind, patient, and hard-working. I was really hoping that you would change your mind and say yes. I mean, how nice would it be to have another woman to talk to at family get-togethers during the holidays."

Then it was my turn to look embarrassed. "I think that is kind of a way down the road... I mean, we just started dating."

"Oh, of course, sorry. Getting a little ahead of myself. I am just so happy to see you and my brother together."

After she left with the boxed goodies in hand, I got to thinking about how genuinely sweet that was. Sandy was concerned about her brother getting hurt, and she was trying to have his back. From the stories Ryan had told me, his family was quite close. Being an only child—that was something I'd always thought I missed out on. And that made me think about Beth; she was the closest thing to a sister I had ever had. Then and there, I decided to stop at Mr. Martin's house on the way home tonight and check up on both of them.

BETH OPENED the door and happily ushered me in. "Thank God you're here. I was just about to pull all my hair out. Dad is driving me crazy! He's a terrible patient."

From down the hall, I could just barely hear Mr. Martin yell, "Don't you listen to her, Other One! Beth is just turning into a Nurse Ratched!"

Upon close inspection, Beth was looking a little worse for wear.

"He is just being impossible, Evie. He won't eat any of the meals that his dietitian approved. And he keeps demanding coffee and turning his nose up at my attempts to keep him healthy!" Her raised voice was obviously meant for Mr. Martin, not me. She began to whisper now. "I mean it, impossible. I worked forever on that egg-white veggie omelet with turkey bacon and whole wheat toast." She pointed at the tray of food resting on the front hall table. "He kept complaining about the diet he has been put on. So, I decided as a treat to surprise him with breakfast for supper."

"And it didn't go over well?" I guessed.

"No, he refuses to eat it. He said that if he eats an omelet, it will be made with the whole egg. He said that egg whites taste like snot. He hates it all, everything from the decaffeinated coffee to the bacon that's 'not really bacon.' He turned his nose up at the whole thing." She was furious but trying not to show it.

"Let me try," I said as I grabbed the tray off the table and headed down the hall to Mr. Martin's bedroom.

"Oh, no—not you too, Other One," he said grumpily as I set the tray down on the side of his bed.

"Are you being stubborn? Doesn't seem like you," I said sarcastically.

"I am not being stubborn. I have always hated healthy food. Why would I want bits in my bread? Or have the caffeine taken out of my coffee? Or turkey instead of pork? How dare they even use the word 'bacon' on the package? And don't even get me started on egg whites. Have you ever eaten an egg white, Other One?"

I answered truthfully. "Only in meringues, like on top of a lemon pie." In retrospect, that probably wasn't the best response.

"Pie? Pie? I will probably never taste pie again, if it's up to Beth and my doctors."

"Beth and your doctors and everybody else that cares about you want to see you healthy again. Back to your old self. And if that means you have to make a few sacrifices, then so be it."

I then placed the tray of food on his lap.

Gus looked up at me, resigned, and slowly he picked up his fork and began to carefully poke at his food, as if there might be a bomb somewhere on the plate that was waiting to explode.

"Why couldn't the sacrifice be a goat or something?" He smiled up at me sadly.

"Just eat, Mr. Martin," I encouraged him. "I am going to go out and catch up with Beth, and I will come back later for this plate. And I expect to find it empty."

BETH HAD SUNK SO FAR into the sofa that I could barely see her when I went looking for her in the living room.

"It's more work than I thought it would be. He's cranky, and the meals are a lot of shopping, prepping, and cooking, and then when he refuses to eat them . . . Argh!"

"It sounds to me like you need a break. And that's why I'm here." I pulled the bottle of wine I'd brought for Beth out of my bag. "Let's start with me pouring us both a glass of this, and you put your feet up." That seemingly settled, I headed to the kitchen in search of a corkscrew.

"It isn't so bad, I guess." Beth's voice floated down the hall. "It's just a lot to get used to. I haven't had to look after anyone but myself for a few years now. And Dad is used to doing everything for himself. He hates being so reliant on me."

I returned with two big-girl glasses of wine.

"You two will settle in with each other. You will make new routines and get used to being in each other's space. He loves you so much—you know that, don't you? He is Gus Martin—a football legend and used to doing everything by himself. Looking after you, not the other way around."

"I know, I know. It's been a tough week. I am really worried about his health. Especially after losing Mom all those years ago. I can't lose him too."

Beth's Mom had been a quiet, sweet woman with carefully done hair and nails, up on the latest women's fashion, like Beth. I had only been friends with Beth for a few years when her mother was diagnosed with Huntington's disease, which initially showed itself as trouble learning new information, and small involuntary body movements. She passed away at the age of forty-five, with Mr. Martin doing the lion's share of helping her with her everyday activities. It had been a long, slow, sad progression, and Mr. Martin had never been quite the same. He never remarried; I'm not sure if he ever even dated. Instead, he threw himself into being the best parent to Beth that he possibly could. I now understand that he was trying to be both mom and dad. And now it was Beth's turn to look after him, and she was taking that job just as seriously.

After a while, I noticed Beth began to relax, and when I checked up on Mr. Martin, true to his word he had eaten his supper, all except for the turkey bacon. He was currently snoring away, so I turned the lights off and took the empty tray into the kitchen. When I returned to the living room, I saw that Beth was also fast asleep on the couch. I pulled a blanket up over her, shut off the lights, and quietly left, locking the door behind me.

Chapter Eighteen

I had finally found Ryan's townhouse. I ended up driving past it twice before I figured out that his house number was actually on one of the posts of his front porch and not above the garage door, like all his neighbours.

When I rang the doorbell, I could hear it ringing in the house, but Ryan didn't appear. I could smell the barbecue from his backyard, so I went around to the side gate and found it unlocked. I walked into the backyard with my fingers crossed that I really did get this right at last, and this really was Ryan's yard that I was barging into. Ryan turned and waved when he saw me coming around the corner. He came over, took the bottle of wine that I had brought, and offered to go inside and get me a glass.

"While I pour you a glass, make yourself comfortable. I'll give you a proper tour inside once the meat is finished on the grill." He motioned to the outdoor furniture placed in a semi-circle next to the barbecue.

The outdoor furniture was very comfortable looking and very male somehow. It was a bit oversized: dark teak furniture topped by deep, black cushions. The backyard was gorgeous; there were no gardens to speak of, just grass. But that grass was so thick and weed-free that it looked like it belonged on a golf course. He had a two-tiered deck with curved sides, and the lower deck had a substantial wooden pergola. It was under this pergola that the furniture was sitting. Out on the grass was a black, ornate iron fire bowl that had stars cut out on the sides, and it got me thinking about how lovely it would look on a dark night when there was a roaring fire inside it. Sitting in front of the fire bowl were two wooden loungers, and looking at them made me wonder if he had ever fallen asleep on those extra-deep black cushions.

"What do you think of my landscaping? It would probably look better with some gardens and colourful flowers, but that just isn't me."

I turned and took another long look around. "It looks amazing. It is beautiful and... very male somehow. I love the dark-stained wood, the black cushioned seating, and the lush green grass. You did a good job. Did you do this work all by yourself?"

"Yes, it was my first try at landscaping. I am pleased with how it turned out. I spend a lot of time out here in the nice weather."

Ryan continued to check on the chicken every ten minutes or so and to baste the meat in some wonderful smelling smoky barbecue sauce. I curled up in one of the armchairs nearest the grill and enjoyed catching up with Ryan about his week while sipping my wine. When the meat was declared finished, I followed him inside the back sliding glass door and into his kitchen. Having an end unit meant that he was lucky enough to have windows down the one side of his house and this, combined with nine-foot ceilings, made his kitchen seem bright and open. Once inside, I could see that he had set two places for us at the dining room table, and he pulled out one of the chairs and invited me to sit.

"Your help is not required. I simply want you to relax and let me bring the food to you."

THE MEAL WAS SIMPLY DELICIOUS, and afterward, I helped him load the dishwasher.

"Now, let me give you that tour I promised you."

The rest of his townhouse was similar in styling to his backyard. A black leather sofa, matching armchair, and dark hardwood furniture throughout, and on every wall black and white nature photography was his only art. I stood in front of one photograph of a mountain; it was striking and somehow almost spiritual.

"Where did you purchase all these photographs? They are incredible—it's almost like you are there."

"I took those photos myself."

"Wow. You are so talented. A contractor, a landscaper, and now a photographer. What other talents do you have hiding up your sleeve?"

"I guess you will have to wait and see." He winked, and then added, "And thank you, by the way.

Photography is a real passion of mine. It really helped me after the divorce. Being out in nature gave me a sense of connection to the world around me. I always came back feeling less stressed and generally more positive."

Once I had been given the entire tour, we circled back to his living room and he encouraged me to have a seat.

"Would you like to have an after-dinner coffee or tea?"

"I would love a tea, herbal if you have it. I tend to drink a lot of caffeine during the day, and I always switch to herbal tea at night."

When Ryan returned with the tea, he found me curled up on his sofa with a soft knitted throw across my legs.

"You look cozy. Is there enough room there for me?" I immediately moved my legs off the sofa so he could sit beside me.

"Thanks." I took the hot mug in both hands.

Ryan sat down beside me and picked up a small remote; suddenly the room was filled with soft music, a slow, sweet country song.

"We could dance later, if you like." Ryan turned to me with a soft smile.

"Dancing? You wouldn't want to dance with me if you had ever *seen* me dance. I have been told my dancing style is, and I quote, ' kind of like a mosquito in a bug zapper.'"

"Now I REALLY want to see you dance."

"You would have to get a few drinks in me first, I think. I don't want to scare you off," I joked.

"I don't scare easily," he said, and then he got an almost pained expression on his face. "I have something I wanted to ask you, speaking of dancing."

"Speaking of dancing? You haven't signed us both up on 'So You Think You Can Dance,' have you?" I teased, wondering if going out dancing was his next date idea.

"Not exactly." He paused for a moment. "My brother Edward—you've never met him, he lives in Ottawa. Well, he has been divorced for five years now. And I wasn't sure if I should even ask you this because we haven't been dating for very long. But... I was wondering. My brother has met a wonderful woman, and he is getting married. I was sent the invitation a while ago, and my whole family was bugging me to RSVP with a plus one. I kept telling them that I wasn't dating anyone, so there was no point. But they insisted that I might be dating someone in six weeks."

I was in shock, I think, and I must have looked it. Ryan looked worried all of a sudden.

"You can say no. I mean, of course, you can say no. The wedding is actually next weekend. And like I said before, I wasn't even going to ask you. I know that I am not giving you any notice. I just thought that I would take a chance because... well because I would love to take you with me. Show you off to my family."

"Family?" I squeaked.

"I know, I know it's too soon. But I could introduce you to them any way you want. I could just introduce you as my friend."

"When next week?"

"Saturday. The rehearsal dinner is on Friday night,

though, and being the best man, I need to be there for that as well. Since the wedding is in Ottawa, which is quite a long drive, I planned to drive up Friday morning. We would be staying over in the hotel for Friday night for the rehearsal and Saturday night for the wedding. We could head home on Sunday."

"I would need to stay overnight? At a hotel? With you?" My brain was trying to keep up.

"Oh please, don't get the wrong idea. I have already inquired about the availability of an extra room at the hotel for you. And just in case you were to say yes, I put a hold on it for you. My treat, of course."

"Can I think about it? I know that you'll obviously need to know as soon as possible. But to be quite honest, you've really surprised me, and I want to sleep on it."

"Of course. Sleep on it—and Evie, I am not trying to rush you into anything. I don't expect you to sleep with me just because we're staying in the same hotel overnight. I would really enjoy your company, and if you came as my date or friend... whatever you want. I know that I will enjoy it so much more with you there. In whatever way that makes you feel comfortable."

"I'm going to think about it. And figure out how that would work with Sara, and talk it over with her as well, of course... but I will let you know tomorrow."

"Thanks for, you know, not freaking out. I went back and forth so many times over even asking you. I know it's too soon, so no hard feelings if you say no."

. . .

THE REST of the night passed in a blur. My mind kept going over it again and again: from being introduced to his entire family; to staying overnight in the same hotel; to how Sara was going to feel about this. I mean, starting to date again was a big enough deal, but this? This was no simple date night.

At the end of the evening, I thanked Ryan for a great meal and a lovely night. Ryan passed me my sweater and purse. When our fingers touched, I felt a buzz, like static electricity, pass between us. I looked up from putting my sweater on to see Ryan standing very close to me. He looked down at me and suddenly reached out. He placed a hand on each side of my face, his thumbs resting gently on my cheeks and his fingers playing softly with the hair on the back of my head. He leaned in and pulled me slowly forward, kissed me softly, and then, when he tilted my head, I opened my lips, and slowly, softly, his tongue began caressing mine. Achingly slow and sweet, he kissed me, tasted me. And I melted into him, kissing him back, lost in this moment, this kiss. He pulled back a little and studied me, his eyes soft and dark, the little lines around them crinkling when he smiled. He took a finger, ran it across my forehead, and tucked a loose curl behind my ear.

"Evie, you are so beautiful." He blew out a breath, long and deep. "We had better say good night before I get too tempted to take you back to the couch and kiss you until you can't see straight."

I sighed, my mouth now incapable of forming words.

"Good night, Evie." He dropped a kiss onto the top of

my head. "Drive safe. I will look forward to hearing from you tomorrow."

And with that, I managed to find my way to the car, and once I turned the key, I immediately turned off the radio, so as not to interfere with replaying that wonderful kiss all the way home.

Chapter Nineteen

The following day, my mind was filled with a raging debate. Should I say no to the wedding invite? Ryan would understand; he said so. Or should I agree to go as his plus one, but with the agreement that I would be introduced as a friend? What would Sara think about this? Was I risking heartbreak for both of us by moving our relationship along too fast? Did I need more time casually dating before being introduced to his entire family, even as just a friend? Hours of this debate, back and forth, round and round, left me feeling mentally exhausted. It was time to bring in reinforcements: I texted Katie for emergency help. I had just finished sending the text when my phone, still in my hand, began to ring.

"I got your S.O.S. I think you had better get your butt over here. Mark is just about to leave for baseball practice, and the kids are at my mom's for the day. The house will be empty, and the tea kettle is already on."

"Thanks, Katie. I will be right over, and I will bring some of my chocolate chip cookies."

"Sounds good. See you soon."

KATIE LIVED in the centre of town, approximately two blocks from The Penthouses. As I drove by the slowly rising condominium, I noticed a new banner stuck across the top corner of the billboard. I stopped my car at the side of the road and rolled down my window for a better look. The sign read, "Phase One is now 50% sold out." I made a mental note to go into the sales office and talk about my interest in one of their units, find out the options for a two-bedroom, and get a price list.

KATIE'S HOUSE was very Katie, which means it was filled with children's artwork on the walls and all over the front of the refrigerator. Her walls were all painted blue, her favourite colour. Each room was a different shade of blue, from navy to baby blue with various shades in between. There were toys scattered everywhere, and I could hear the dryer going and the smell of clean laundry in the air. Katie's house was one of those houses where, when you got inside, you breathed a sigh of relief because you just instantly felt at home. Katie was in some comfortable-looking purple velour loungewear, and she yelled from the kitchen for me to come on in and bring the chocolate chip cookies with me.

"Evie, Evie, Evie, have a seat." She pointed at the kitchen table. "The doctor is in."

"In this scenario, you are the doctor? Wow. Physician, heal thyself."

"Enough out of you, Evie. Now spill it! What's going on? What's the emergency?"

"I have to talk to somebody about this... I just don't know what to do."

Katie made a waving gesture with her hand as if to say, get to the point.

"Ryan asked me last night if I would consider being his plus one at his brother's wedding."

"Is that all? I thought this was a real emergency. Like you found out that he lied, and he's still married, and you're about to have his love child."

That made me snort tea out of my nose. "Love child?! Seriously?"

"Well then, what's the big deal? Go to the wedding with him."

"The wedding is in Ottawa, which is a five-hour drive away."

"So you... what... get car sick? You think he won't look at you the same after you barf all over the inside of his truck?"

"Very funny. No, it's five hours away, and he is the best man, and that means that he has to be there the day before for the rehearsal, and the wedding itself isn't taking place until late in the afternoon, so that means we have to stay over in a hotel. For not one, but two nights."

"Oh." This wasn't a good sign from Katie; she was never at a loss for words.

"What should I do? I have gone over and over this in my mind, and I don't know what to do."

"What do you want to do?"

"What do you mean? I just explained that I don't *know* what I want to do."

"No, you didn't. You said that, basically, you have overthought this for hours. But what I want to know is, without any debate or mental pros or cons, just tell me what you want to do?"

I took a deep breath and said, "I want to go."

"Why?"

"Because I enjoy spending time with Ryan. And... I am starting to think that maybe Ryan is worth making extra room in my heart for."

"Then you go."

"It's not that simple."

"Tell me why it can't be that simple."

"Well, what about Sara? How's she going to react? Do I want to meet Ryan's entire family this soon? I know he has booked us separate hotel rooms. But what if it gets weird staying overnight at the same hotel? Ryan said that he could introduce me as a friend if that made me feel more comfortable. But I don't even know the right word for what we are together. A girlfriend at my age? I am hardly a girl. Significant other? Too soon in the relationship. Partner? Ditto."

"One, I think that Sara will be able to handle you going to an out-of-town wedding with the man you are dating. Especially when you tell her that he is the best man and that Ryan has booked you separate rooms. Two, I don't think there has been a relationship since the beginning of time that doesn't run the risk of becoming weird with the partner's family after a breakup or even a divorce. That's just part of taking the risk. Three, Ryan has had the forethought to book two hotel rooms. That says to me that he is being respectful of you wanting to take things slow. Four, I think he should touch you on the arm or the small of your back, or maybe hold your hand and introduce you as Evie. Only the densest person would not understand that you mean something to each other. And what that something is, well, that's none of their business." Katie reached for another chocolate chip cookie from the plate in front of us. "Oh, and for what it's worth. I think that love is always worth taking a risk."

"I don't know how you do it, Katie. You just have this way of calming the circus in my head. Thank you."

"Just call me the ringmaster, or would that be ringmistress? Now, eat some of these cookies for me before I eat them all and make myself sick."

SARA CAME HOME from her volleyball game in a great mood later that afternoon.

"Let me guess. You won, right?"

"We crushed them. We made them all go crying home to their mommas."

"Oh, goodie! I love it when the 'fruit of my loins' crushes other girls."

"'Fruit of your loins'?! Gross! You are just so cringy sometimes."

"Okay, I will give you that one. How about the twinkle in my eye?"

"How about we stop this before it gets worse?"

"Fine. Party pooper. After you shower and change, I was wondering if we could have a little chat?"

"Sure, Mom. As soon as I get myself all cleaned up, I will come back down, and we can talk. Nothing's wrong, is it?"

"No, nothing to worry about. We'll talk when you come back downstairs."

SARA CAME BOUNDING down the stairs with her still-wet hair brushed and falling heavy over her shoulders. She smelled like her shampoo, kind of a beachy coconut fragrance. And for a moment, she looked so much like her father that my heart squeezed. She must not be planning on going out anymore today because she had her favourite onesie pyjamas on, complete with her fluffy pink slippers. She ran straight for the refrigerator.

"I'm starving. Is there anything to eat?"

"You are looking at a full refrigerator. How could there be nothing to eat?"

"You know what I mean. I mean food that doesn't have to be... you know... cooked in order to be eaten."

"How about I make you a grilled cheese sandwich?"

"Sounds yummy. Now, what did you want to chat about?" Sara made herself comfortable on one of the leather stools at the kitchen island and put her face in her hands, watching me make her favourite sandwich. I tried to condense the question of attending the wedding to the bare bones, exactly as Katie did for me. I was letting her know that Ryan's brother was getting married in Ottawa and that he was the best man. The fact that it was taking place over the course of a couple of days would mean that we would need to stay overnight. And that Ryan and I would be in two separate hotel rooms.

Sara took it all in very nonchalantly. "Oh, that sounds like fun. You love weddings. You especially love all the dancing at weddings. I remember the last wedding that you, Dad, and I attended. Dad's cousin Lilly's wedding, right? I remember taking a video of you dancing. It was so hilarious. I remember showing my friends at school, and everyone wanted me to send them the video. You almost went viral!"

"I do remember that. Hard to forget when your dancing moves are being critiqued and laughed at by all the teens in town. So... you are okay with this?"

"Yes, of course. It's not that big a deal. When is this wedding, anyway?"

"Well, that's the other thing. It's next weekend. We will have to figure out how that's going to work."

"Actually, next weekend is perfect."

"How so?"

"I am babysitting overnight for Mr. and Mrs. Smyth on Friday night while they go to a concert in the city."

"What about Saturday night, though?"

"I could ask Olivia to come over here, and we could binge-watch all the Twilight movies."

"When I talked to Katie today, she said that she could look in on you, and make sure everything's okay."

"She can if that makes you feel better, Mom. But you know that, come fall, I might be living in residence in British Columbia, right? How will you look in on me then? You will have to trust that you raised me to look after myself and know that if I need your help, you are always a phone call away."

"You are getting a little ahead of yourself. Look, I know you're eighteen, but you're still my baby."

"Yes, I know... I'm the 'fruit of your loins'." She cringed visibly at having said those words. "Sure, have Katie check up on us. And ask her when she does if she could possibly bring us a couple of her almond milk lattes with a shot of vanilla?"

I guess that was the end of the conversation because she then began to tell me all about her volleyball team's victory. All while dunking her grilled cheese sandwich in a huge mound of ketchup.

Chapter Twenty

I called Ryan to let him know that I'd decided to go to his brother's wedding and to find out all the little details I should know.

"I'm so glad that you decided to come. My brother is a great guy, and his bride is so nice, you are really going to like them both. I think that this wedding is going to be a lot of fun." Ryan's voice sounded kind of stuffy.

"Your voice—you haven't come down with a cold? Have you?"

"It seems like it. But I am sure I will be healthy by Friday, which will give me five more days to recover. You're not starting to feel run down, are you? I was thinking about that kiss on Friday night and hoping I didn't give you this cold."

I pictured that kiss in my mind, his soft lips, how he smelled, my fingers playing softly in the silky hair at the back of his neck. I sighed. "No, not me. I'm the picture of health. Must be all my 'clean living.'"

Ryan snorted at that. "Clean living now includes tons of caffeine, cookies, and wine, does it?"

"You do clean living your way... I'll do it mine."

Ryan laughed. "I like your way better."

"Of course you do—you're not stupid. Now, about this wedding. Can you give me the hotel address? It's for Sara, just in case of an emergency. Oh, and what do you think your brother and his fiancée would like for a wedding gift? Let's face it—I don't have much time to go shopping before the wedding on Saturday."

"I have already bought them a big gift, and I will just add your name to the card."

"If you're sure that would be okay."

"No problem. What else do you need to know?"

I found out that, yes, the wedding was taking place in the hotel itself. No, he wouldn't accept any money towards the gift or the hotel room. And yes, he was planning on taking off work on Friday to have enough time to get there for the start of the afternoon rehearsal. I told him that I needed to do the café baking on Friday morning, but since that was usually done by eight, we could leave any time after that.

I DIDN'T HAVE enough time to go dress or shoe shopping before Friday. Luckily, I have quite an impressive shoe collection. As for a suitable dress, my fancy dresses hanging in the closet were hardly worn out from overuse.

In the end, I decided on the safest bet. A pretty, slim-fitting little black dress with a plunging neckline that was made respectable by the overlaying of some

Evie's Haven

beautiful black lace. The shoes I chose were high-heeled little ankle boots in a fire engine shade of red. All of that was topped off with a red silk clutch-style purse decorated with various coloured silk flowers and pearl beads.

TRUE TO HIS usual style of always being right on time, Ryan pulled into my driveway at nine on Friday morning. He helped me with my large suitcase and questioned why my bag was so heavy as he struggled to lift it into the back of the truck.

"It would be bad luck not to bring my lucky rocks to the wedding," I teased. The real reason being that I'd brought more changes of shoes and clothes than was strictly necessary. I felt pretty nervous about meeting the rest of Ryan's family, and looking my best would boost my confidence.

We drove for a while in comfortable silence while finishing our fast-food breakfast and the take-out coffee I had brought from the café. When we finished eating, we began talking about our childhoods and what we were like in high school, then college, and our very first job afterwards.

I told Ryan about meeting John in a pub around the corner from the university we had both attended. How John had seen me there with my friends and bought me a drink to get my attention. He then proceeded to go back to that pub every night for two weeks until he happened to see me there again, so that he could ask me for my number. He said he had gotten my name the first night, but it wasn't until after I left that he realized he hadn't asked for my number.

I told him that John and I moved in together within a few months of meeting and that we had been inseparable since then.

Ryan was an excellent listener, and I could tell that he was genuinely interested in what I was saying. He asked some questions here and there, but only to clarify some aspects of the story, not to knock me off my train of thought or try to steer the conversation in another direction. He just had this way of making you feel heard and validated, and... just so... interesting to him.

I asked him if he would mind telling me about his ex-wife Debbie.

"We met at a house party. I don't even remember whose place it was at, a friend of a friend, I think. Anyways, Debbie was there with a couple of friends, and she accidentally spilled her drink all over me. She was walking by me, and she suddenly tripped."

I laughed. "Quite the meet cute!"

"I had already noticed her from across the room. She was standing there, talking with a group of friends, and she had long, curly, red hair and the most striking hazel eyes. Anyway... she apologized for spilling her drink all over me and she offered to go to the bathroom and get me a towel to try and sop up all the beer from my shirt. But it wasn't the way she looked or her apology that made me fall in love with her. It was her laughter while she was trying to apologize that got to me. It was the most joyful laugh I had ever heard. And as they say, 'that was that.'

We dated for about a year before I asked her to marry me."

Ryan told me that the first two years were happy ones; they were working hard to save up enough money for a down payment on a house. But once they had the house, Debbie was eager to start trying for a baby. Debbie had come from a large family, and she couldn't wait for them to start a family of their own.

"That first year of trying, we didn't let ourselves get too disappointed; we knew these things can take some time. But after a year and a half of trying, we decided to make an appointment with a fertility specialist. I won't bore you with the nitty-gritty... long story short, it turned out that there were fertility problems. More than that, it was the doctor's opinion that we would not be able to have a child of our own."

I reached over and gave Ryan's shoulder a soft squeeze. He turned to look at me for just a fleeting moment and gave me a small, sad smile. Then he cleared his throat.

"We explored alternatives like adoption, and Debbie initially agreed to start the process. But after a while she sat me down and told me she had changed her mind and didn't want to pursue it anymore. I tried countless times to have a conversation about those other options, but Debbie just shut me down." Ryan then took a long, slow breath. "I saw this was starting to take a toll on our marriage. I asked her to come with me to couples counselling, but Debbie stopped going after a few sessions. After that, she seemed to throw herself into work, and after a while, she began acting like her old self again. I figured that she just must have needed a break from the whole baby idea. It was just so nice to see her laughing again."

I nodded sympathetically.

"Then one day I came home from work to find Debbie sitting at the kitchen table waiting for me. She told me she had been having an affair with a man at work and... she was three months pregnant with his child."

Ryan was silent for a moment, and when he continued, his voice had a quiet, resigned tone to it. "In retrospect, I probably should have seen the signs. Debbie hadn't wanted to have sex in months. She was always too tired or she claimed she had to get up early the next morning. I was concerned about it at the time, but it was so good to see her back to her old self, I decided not to push the issue."

It was obviously very painful to Ryan that Debbie seemed to move on from their marriage very quickly after that. She was overjoyed to be pregnant after all their fertility issues, which somehow seemed to overshadow any possibilities for guilt or remorse over having carried on a six-month affair with a coworker.

In the end, the divorce was a contentious, long, drawn-out affair, with Debbie always claiming that he owed her more than what was agreed on in court. She fought him over every piece of furniture, every knick-knack, even heirloom pieces and photographs from his side of the family.

"Worst of all," Ryan added, "Before the divorce was even finalized, she had already moved in with the baby's father. Then after the divorce was finalized, Debbie remarried as quickly as the law allowed."

I didn't know what to say. I slid my hand over and squeezed his leg. He lifted one hand off the wheel and, without speaking, he gently entwined our fingers. We sat silently, holding hands and listening to the radio.

ONE MINUTE I was dreaming about making the world's biggest muffin and was just about to accept a Guinness World Record for it when something startled me awake. Ryan had shut off the truck and we were sitting outside a large hotel in Ottawa. I blinked a few times, trying to make sense of this.

"Wakey-wakey, Evie. You slept the rest of the way here."

"I see that," I said sleepily while trying to stretch my arms over my head.

Ryan came around and opened my door. "You were snoring a little. You must have been exhausted." He was smiling, genuinely enjoying himself.

"Well, I have been up since five this morning to have enough time to finish the baking at the café. So yes, I admit to being really tired. But no, I don't snore."

Ryan had the unmitigated gall to laugh at that statement. "Um, Okay, Evie, whatever you say."

"Whatever I say? You bet it's whatever I say because I don't snore. I know because John would have mentioned that to me at some point. Don't you think?" I accepted his arm and jumped down with as much dignity as possible.

"So what you are saying is that John was hard of

hearing?" Ryan was still smiling at me, a huge joyful smile.

"Hard of hearing?" I muttered to myself. "I'll give you hard of hearing."

"What was that, Evie? I didn't catch what you just said."

I turned around and smiled back at him. "Oh, I guess that's because you're hard of hearing?" Game, set, match. I smiled smugly.

"I guess you're right. One trip in the car with you snoring away and I'm apparently beginning to lose my hearing. But twenty years sleeping right beside that snoring? It's a miracle that John didn't require a hearing aid."

"You are infuriating." I began to stomp off in the direction of the hotel lobby.

Ryan caught up to me and grabbed my arm to turn me around. Then, to my surprise, he kissed me. Right there in the hotel parking lot, soft and sweet and hungry. "You can snore all you want, drool even," he said when he finally pulled back from the kiss to look into my eyes. "You were the cutest sleeper that I have ever seen. I hated to shut the truck off and wake you."

"Well, in that case... maybe... only occasionally... when I'm really tired. I might... snore a little bit." I conceded, and I reached up on tiptoes to kiss him again. When we emerged from that second kiss a while later, it was to the sound of someone directly behind us clearing their throat.

Chapter Twenty-One

"**M**om and Dad, let me introduce Evie." Ryan hugged his mom and shook his father's hand. He didn't seem the least bit embarrassed to be caught kissing in the parking lot. I, on the other hand, was feeling a blush blooming up my neck and across my cheeks.

"So nice to meet you, Mr. and Mrs. Sullivan." I extended my hand towards them, trying to keep it from trembling.

"Oh, you can call us Judith and Frank. It's so nice to meet you finally, Evie. I have heard such great things," Judith said as she warmly shook my offered hand.

Frank took it one step further and reached out to give me a friendly, enveloping hug. "Welcome, Evie," he said, stepping back to smile at me with his warm, crinkling eyes.

"Thank you," I managed to say as I smoothed my hair.

It was probably a mess after sleeping in the truck for hours.

Frank and Judith had just arrived as well, I realized, when I saw the large, wheeled suitcase at Frank's feet.

Ryan was the spitting image of Frank, tall and dark with large, warm eyes, although Frank's hair now had more grey in it than brown. Watching them all talking, I also decided that Ryan had his mother's full lips and her laugh.

It seemed like it had been decided that everyone was going to check in and unpack, and then we were all going to meet in the lobby bar to have, as Frank put it, a quiet drink before the chaos.

Ryan picked up our keys from the front desk and insisted on carrying my bag to my room. The rooms ended up being on the same floor but on opposite ends of the hall from each other. Ryan dropped me off in my room, wheeled my heavy bag inside, and set it on the luggage rack in the closet. He looked around the large room.

"Sorry about not being able to get you a king bed. Although, I thought you might like having the two queen beds instead. This way, you can set your outfits out on one bed and sleep in the other."

How does this man know how my mind works? Spooky!

"It looks great to me. It's actually huge and bright for a hotel room, and that coffee machine is state of the art."

That made Ryan chuckle. "Of course you *would* notice the coffee machine first." Then he added, "My room has one king bed, so if you want, we could switch. It doesn't matter to me."

"That's nice of you to offer, but I think this room suits me just fine."

And with that settled, Ryan left me to freshen up, and we planned to meet down in the lobby bar in twenty minutes. I took the opportunity to call Sara to make sure everything was going alright and double-check that she had the hotel's address and Ryan's cell phone number, just in case my phone battery died. After that call was successfully completed, I gave Katie a call at the café.

"What are you doing calling me on your weekend away? You've only been gone a few hours."

"Just calling to make sure you aren't rushed off your feet. Because I could call in one of the weekend students if you need it. And... also to remind you to check up on Sara tomorrow."

"It's busy this afternoon, but I can make it through. And of course I won't forget to check up on Sara tomorrow night. In fact, I am planning on bringing them the lattes they asked for, as well as some popcorn. Maybe I can sweet talk them into letting me stay for a while to watch a movie with them. Now... get off the phone and go and have a fun weekend with Ryan. Remember, I expect a full report on Monday morning. Make notes if you have to. I want all the juicy details."

"Okay, Katie, I will take lots of pictures. And thank you. Having you check up on Sara for me makes me feel so much better about this weekend."

"Not a problem, Evie. Go have fun, and that's an order."

. . .

I MET Ryan and his parents down in the lobby bar; Ryan had a glass of white wine waiting for me. After a few minutes, I saw a familiar figure coming toward us.

"Sandy, so good to see you. Especially outside of work." I stood up to give her a quick hug.

"If I get my wish, I'll see you at all my family functions." Sandy winked at me.

"Err . . . Thanks, Sandy."

We had about an hour before the rehearsal began, and the time passed quickly. I found out from Judith and Frank that they had heard great things about my café through Sandy, and they planned on coming in to see what all the fuss was about. They were warm and friendly and seemed genuinely interested in getting to know me. I had worried that getting to know Ryan's parents might be awkward, but my worries were unfounded.

THE REHEARSAL STARTED in the ballroom right on time, and that's where I got to meet Ryan's brother Edward and his fiancée, Kelly. They looked about my age and seemed very much in love. It was Edward's second marriage and Kelly's first. Kelly told me that she had been in a long-term relationship that ended a few years ago. She had two teenagers from that relationship: a fifteen-year-old girl and an eighteen-year-old boy.

My worries about how I was going to be introduced were unfounded. Ryan introduced me as Evie, and just as Katie had predicted, no one asked any further questions about our relationship status. After all the introductions were made and the minister arrived, it was time for the rehearsal to start. I felt a little like a third wheel, but I thought this would be more entertaining to watch than television alone in my room.

Watching Ryan's family and close friends interact with an outsider's eyes left me with a warm feeling. Their good-natured teasing and affection for each other were nice to see.

After the successful rehearsal, a dinner followed in the hotel's main restaurant. The meal was excellent and the wine flowed freely. But a full stomach and a few glasses of wine later, I was becoming aware that my nap hadn't been enough sleep to keep the day from catching up with me. Ryan had noticed me fighting to keep my eyes open.

"Evie, you should go up to bed. This has been a long day for you. Ed said that there is going to be a late-night guys' card game in the bar afterward, so you might as well get a good night's sleep. Tomorrow is going to be a very long day."

After I made my excuses and said good night to everyone, Ryan told the table he was going to walk me up to my room, but that he would be right back.

As SOON AS the elevator doors closed, Ryan pulled me towards him and gave me a long kiss.

"You were so lovely with my family. So patient, answering all their questions as if those questions hadn't been asked again and again today. I have been watching you all afternoon and biding my time to get you alone."

Ryan smelled so nice, and I found myself snuggling up against his warm chest. "It is so nice to meet the rest of your family, especially your parents and your brother Ed. After hearing about them from you, I felt like I already knew them." I kissed him back. "Thanks for seeing me up to my room. You are always such a gentleman."

Ryan lifted his hands and cradled my face, gazing into my eyes. "A gentleman, huh? So obviously my reputation hasn't preceded me." He swooped me back into a dramatic dip and kissed me again. Then he pulled back and brushed his lips on my temple down to the tip of my nose and finally, softly, and fully, on my mouth. He then gave me a slow, sweet smile and pulled me into his arms.

I sighed and blew out a long, slow breath. "You make it hard for me to think," I whispered.

"I know what you mean. I find it hard to think when you are around too. Especially when I have you in my arms." He took a step away and let his arms slowly fall. "But I promised to see you safely to your room." He sighed. "I know that you are almost asleep on your feet. And when you feel ready to take things further... I want you to be fully awake and present for that."

I nodded in agreement. I was not trusting my own voice.

Ryan took me to my door, and we made plans to meet the following day for breakfast.

I usually have problems going to sleep in a hotel, but tonight I dropped off as soon as my head hit the pillow.

Chapter Twenty-Two

I was coughing on my first mouthful of coffee for the day; luckily, I hadn't started getting dressed yet. I would hate to be dressed to the nines and smelling of cold coffee all day.

By the time I got to the lobby for breakfast, I was dressed to impress. I had even managed to create a cheater French roll updo with my hair. As I rounded the corner, I caught my first look at Ryan, all dressed up. He was talking to someone and hadn't seen me yet. I took a moment to catch my breath and enjoy the view. He was beautiful to look at, especially in a tuxedo. His beard was freshly trimmed, and from this angle you could see the long, straight lines of his nose and his jaw. The tuxedo pants seemed to enhance the muscular legs underneath. Suddenly he turned and saw me, and he smiled a slow, sweet smile. Then he mimed a whistle and used his hands to outline a woman's figure in the air. I chuckled softly to myself, the quiet moment gone.

. . .

THE WEDDING itself was an intimate affair, with a minister officiating at a short service in a smaller room just off the hotel ballroom. Judith and Frank asked me to sit with them, so I got to have a front-row seat for the ceremony. Ryan was the best man, and with Sandy as a bridesmaid, all their children were part of the wedding. Judith and Frank looked incredibly proud as they watched them all taking part in Edward's wedding. Judith reached over and grabbed my hand to squeeze it when the minister announced Ed and Kelly were now officially man and wife.

RYAN WASN'T able to sit with me during the reception dinner, as he was seated at the head table. But Ryan was keeping an eye on me from afar; he seemed to be checking that I wasn't left alone or feeling uncomfortable. He didn't need to worry, though; I wasn't left alone to flounder. Ryan's parents kept me company and introduced me to all the extended family and friends. They made me feel like an important part of their family.

When the dinner and all the speeches were over, Ryan came and sat with me at the table. It was an open bar, Ryan was drinking whiskey, and I was enjoying tall flutes of Prosecco. He was laughing and trading old stories of a misspent youth that included Sandy, Ed, and himself. A while later, and a few drinks in, Ryan asked me to dance. Luckily it was a slow dance, so I knew I wouldn't embarrass myself.

Ryan smelled of his aftershave and faintly of the smoky whiskey he had been drinking. I couldn't help myself; unabashedly, I snuggled into his warm chest. He was solid and made me feel safe in his arms. When he kissed me tenderly on the top of my head, I felt something else: loved. It had been so long since I'd felt loved in that way. I didn't want the dance to end. The DJ played three slow songs in a row, and Ryan and I didn't leave each other's arms. Sometime during the third song, Ryan leaned down and began to kiss me right there on the dance floor in front of his whole family and all their friends. Maybe I should have felt embarrassed, but I didn't. I tilted my face up at him and kissed him back with an intensity that matched his own.

Ryan seemed to realize that people were staring at us when the song ended.

"I would like to kiss you, but maybe somewhere more . . . private. I hope that I didn't embarrass you."

A blush was creeping across my cheeks. "I am as guilty of that show we just put on as you are," I said, and I grabbed his hand to walk off the dance floor.

THE RIDE UP the elevator to our floor was very quiet. The air seemed charged, and with such a small space, I wondered if this was how spontaneous combustion happened. If it did actually happen? At all? Ever? I shook my head and told myself to stop drifting and focus. Focus on that gorgeous man standing so close to me. So close that I could feel his breath, and I swear that I could hear his heart beating. Except I knew that it was simply the echo of my own heart hammering away.

All of a sudden I was aware, in that prickly hair on the back of your neck kind of way, that he was staring at me. I turned and looked up at him. He was looking at me with the biggest, darkest eyes I had ever seen. Right then, it struck me that I wanted to touch him. And I want him to touch me. Even more than just . . . touch. I want to feel alive with him, go up to my room, shut the world out, and just be with him. Should I? Touch him? Let him touch me? Could I shut out all the other thoughts in my head? Was this the Prosecco talking? I knew that I wasn't drunk and that these feelings weren't coming from alcohol. I just wanted Ryan; I wanted him badly.

The elevator dinged, and the doors opened. Almost as if Ryan had heard my inner monologue, he reached down with his large, warm hand and grabbed mine. Together we headed down the hall in the direction of his room.

When we reached Ryan's room, he fumbled in his pocket for his key card. "Come in for a nightcap with me?"

I hesitated but just for a moment. "Sure, lead the way."

He held the door open for me to walk in first. The light switch wasn't difficult to find, and suddenly that large king-sized bed seemed to fill the entire room.

"Have a seat. I'll get us some cups from the bathroom."

I looked around the room. The only choices for

seating were a hard-backed wooden chair that faced the desk, or the bed. It seemed too awkward, formal somehow, to sit on that chair. So I smoothed my dress over my knees and sat on the bed. On the very **edge** of the bed.

Ryan grabbed a bottle of wine from the refrigerator and a small bottle of whiskey from the desk. "I am hoping wine will be okay. I don't have any Prosecco."

"Of course, yes, please."

He poured our two drinks into the glass tumblers he had found in the bathroom. He handed me mine, and after pouring himself a whiskey, he sat down beside me on the edge of the bed. He was sitting so close that our thighs were pressed together.

"Cheers." He clinked my glass.

"To Ed and Kelly." I took a sip and tried to swallow it without choking. My mouth suddenly seemed so dry.

"Evie?"

I turned to see him staring at me again. This time with an intensity, a fierce longing that I hadn't seen in years. It was just my name. But that was all I needed to hear. I just stopped thinking, and I reached a hand up to his face and laid my palm along his jaw. I gazed into his eyes for probably only a second, but it felt like minutes had gone by. Then I leaned forward, and I kissed him. There was no thought, none. I was just feeling the crisp hairs of his beard under my palm, the warmth of his skin, and the softness of his lips.

"Evie." This time it wasn't a question. He opened his mouth, and with the tip of his tongue he swept across the seam of my lips, tasting me. I sighed and opened my mouth; he took the opportunity to sweep his tongue inside. I could taste him, which was more intoxicating than anything I had drunk at the wedding. I pulled away for just a moment, and my decision was made. I reached out, grabbed his glass, put both our glasses on the bedside table and turned back towards him.

"I haven't been with anyone since John."

"Do you want this? I don't want to pressure you into doing something you're not ready for. But if you're sure, I want you to know that I want you. I want you to stay with me tonight."

I couldn't deny him. I couldn't fool myself; I knew this was what I wanted too. I felt consumed with this need for him. I reached out and entwined my fingers around the soft hair at the back of his neck and kissed him. I got utterly lost in kissing him. Time stopped; there was only him. His smell filled my nose, and his touch burned through my dress. I had the sudden need to touch him, all of him.

Chapter Twenty-Three

"Lie back," I said.

He didn't hesitate; he pushed himself back on the bed and laid down. Before I climbed onto the bed, I unzipped and pulled my dress over my head and kicked off my shoes. I let my body rest on top of him, feeling his heat. Then, slowly, I unbuttoned and rid him of his shirt while he undid his bow tie. His chest now bared, I swept my hands across him. I used them, like a blind person would, to see. His muscular chest, the crispy sprinkling of hair between his nipples that tapered down towards his belt. When my fingers reached his belt, he quickly unbuckled it and, together, we rid him of his pants. I lay on him again with my head on his chest, breathing him in.

My fingers began to inch under the waistband of his underwear, and I looked up into his eyes. He lifted himself so that I could get his underwear off, and I threw them on the floor beside the bed. My gaze travelled to an impressive erection. He was beautifully made, and his naked body made me want to take my time and enjoy this feast for my eyes. He watched me staring at his body, and he smiled at me.

Suddenly, I moved up his body, my hands holding me over him. I kissed him with all my pent-up longing, need, and loneliness. Then, he flipped me over so that it was me now on my back.

"Now, it's my turn."

He unclasped my bra and had my underwear off so quickly I was unsure exactly how he had done it. It seemed kind of like a magic trick. The one where they remove the tablecloth while leaving all the dishes and utensils intact. But I... no longer felt intact. I was fragmenting, melting. He slid down my body softly, kissing his way down.

"Your breasts are just too perfect," he said as he pulled one pebbled nipple into his warm mouth and gently sucked. He continued his journey down my body. "Your belly button is so cute." He circled it with one finger, dipping inside. When he came to my soft pubic hair, he hesitated. "With your history of giving people nicknames... I am just guessing here, but what do you call her?" He smiled wolfishly up at me.

"Her Highness?"

"How exciting—I've never met royalty before." He then lowered his mouth and softly kissed my mound. After a while, I realised that I was panting and pleading. "Don't stop, don't stop."

I came hard, so hard that for a moment I thought I had maybe popped a rib. But what's a pulled rib compared to the complete wash of pleasure that flattened me into that bed? I might have made some sounds. I wasn't sure, and I didn't care either.

He climbed back up my body. His weight against me felt wonderful. He kissed me long and deep. I reached down and touched him. Touched the silky soft, warm shaft. His breath hissed through his teeth as I gently squeezed him. He allowed me to continue running my hand up and down his shaft for a few minutes, and then his hand stilled mine.

"I can't handle too much more of that." He pushed himself back to grab a condom from inside the drawer of the bedside table. He looked down at me without speaking. Then, using both his hands, he pushed my thighs apart, wide. He loomed over me again, and at the exact moment his lips touched mine with a deep searching kiss, slowly—achingly slow—he entered me.

We found a rhythm all our own. Our bodies fit together perfectly, his hips rocking against mine, and I found myself wishing I could stop time.

He came with a shuddering sigh. When he laid down beside me, our sweat cooling, hearts still racing, he traced my face with one finger, looking deep into my eyes and saying my name softly over and over.

After a while, I rolled over onto my stomach and rested my chin on my hands. Ryan rolled towards me and playfully grabbed my bountiful backside.

"Your ass is the most beautiful ass I have ever seen. So plump and round. I want to give it a love bite."

"A love bite?" I was shocked but also a little intrigued.

"Not now," he said as he pulled me towards him to

spoon. "There will be lots of time for that later." He pulled the covers over us both and snuggled in.

The last thing I can remember thinking before sleep took me under was, *Later . . . there would be a later.*

IN THE MORNING there was light coming in the window, and just for a moment, I was confused about where I was. Then I felt a large, warm arm hug me into his embrace; the evening before seemed like a beautiful dream. A dream of tangled arms and legs, feeling completely cherished and connected. His arm then travelled down my side to cup my bare behind. I had forgotten I'd fallen asleep naked, and apparently so had Ryan, because a certain part of his anatomy had woken up and was now poking me in the back. I turned into his embrace so we were face to face. He had an expression that read totally satisfied and relaxed.

"Good morning, sunshine," he said as he pulled me closer to his amazingly warm body.

"Good morning to you." I snuggled closer to him and breathed him in.

"Last night was amazing." He began to nuzzle and kiss my neck.

"Yes, it was... amazing," I managed to say while I could still speak. My body was still singing from last night, and I felt like a woman who had been lost in the desert, dying of thirst, who had just had her first sip of water and was anticipating her second.

"Let's work up an appetite for breakfast, shall we?" he asked, all while nuzzling, kissing, and sucking his way down my body. I didn't need to speak; my body answered for me. My body answered, *yes, yes, please.*

AFTER BREAKFAST, we said our good-byes to everyone, got in the truck and headed home.

"Thank you for inviting me. I had a lot of fun, and I loved meeting your family. They are really wonderful, warm people."

"No, thank *you* for agreeing to come. You impressed my mom, you know."

"I did?" That surprised me.

"Yes. Last night just before the dancing started, my mother pulled me aside and said, 'She's a keeper, you know that, don't you?'. Apparently, you have a fan."

"Aww, that is so sweet. Tell your mother I'm a big fan of hers as well. Both of your parents were so welcoming and friendly, introducing me to everyone and ensuring I was never left alone. They are quite lovely, you know."

"I think that you should tell her that yourself. My mom said she wants to have a big family barbecue in a couple of weeks, and she told me in no uncertain terms to invite you. Well, you and Sara. Mom is looking forward to meeting her."

My eyes teared up at that. "Of course we will come. Just let me know the date."

I REALIZED halfway home that I hadn't checked in on Sara at all yesterday. That thought would usually have me gripped with panic. But today, it didn't. I just knew that I had raised a confident, resourceful girl who would have contacted Katie or me if she had run into trouble. I couldn't wait to get home, hear all about her weekend, and show her all the amazing photographs I had taken at the wedding.

We made great time getting home, and the ride was a relaxed one. We filled the hours easily, talking about some of the people I had met at the wedding, and he tried to explain who he was related to and how. We talked about the wedding and about his brother and his new wife. We held hands most of the way home, and a few times, I could see out of the corner of my eye him sneaking glances at me. I think I smiled all the way home. I probably looked kind of maniacal, but that smile on my face was one of pure happiness. And one that I hoped was here to stay.

Chapter Twenty-Four

B right and early Monday morning at the café, I was inspired by the wedding to create a new cupcake. I was going to call it "Evie's Fountain of Chocolate Cupcake." I started with my mother's old chocolate cake recipe. After the cupcakes had cooled, I piped creamy chocolate fudge frosting into the centre of each one. I piped that same frosting in circles on the top and garnished it with chocolate-dipped strawberries, raspberries, and pineapple pieces. I ended up eating only chocolate-covered fruit for my breakfast. Well, that and copious amounts of caffeine. But that fact is nobody's business but my own.

Katie blew into the kitchen and threw her purse on the table. "So? I've been waiting for these details you promised me. I was hoping maybe you would phone me last night."

"Sorry, Katie. It was a long day of driving, and by the

time I got home and talked with Sara about her weekend, I could hardly see straight. I went straight to bed."

"That's okay, it was quite a busy weekend for you. Now, no detail is too small to leave out. Dish."

At that exact moment, the bell over the front door chimed, telling us the first customer of the day had arrived.

"Drat. We will talk later. And remember—the juicier, the better. I don't mind if you need to embellish it. In fact, it's encouraged." Katie said that last part over her shoulder while she headed around the corner to the front counter.

During the first quiet moment of the day, Katie cornered me behind the counter. "You don't need to tell me that you slept with Ryan. I already know." She then smiled widely and winked at me.

"How in the world could you possibly know that? Are you some kind of sex clairvoyant?"

"Yes. Yes, I am. If you must know, it's that satisfied smile that has been on your face all day. Even after that crabby older man complained about waiting too long for his coffee at lunchtime. I mean, he has been retired for a zillion years now. You don't want to have to wait in line to get your coffee? Then don't come in during the lunchtime rush, Duh! No... no. I am not going off on a tangent about that right now. Back to you and Ryan getting busy. Your turn."

"Getting busy? How old are you again? And who said that we got up to anything?"

Katie pressed her fingers to the side of her head. "Madame Katie sees all. She sees that you and Ryan definitely were 'knocking boots,' 'jumping each other's bones' or... shall I go on?"

"Ugh, please don't. Just because I had a great weekend and I happen to be in a very good mood doesn't have to mean I had sex."

"But you did."

"Okay, Madame Katie, for once you are right, I *did* sleep with him, but that doesn't mean that—"

"I KNEW it. I just knew it. I mean, that smile on your face just screams, 'I just had my tingle untangled.'"

"What in the hell are you even talking about? My tingle untangled? I had sex, alright? Can we leave it alone now?"

"Not just sex. Really great sex."

"Yes, Madame Katie, really great sex, mind-blowing, bones melting, fireworks exploding sex! Are you happy now?"

From behind me came a deep male voice. "Oh, it sounds like someone is *very* happy."

Ugh, it was Trouble. Of all the men to overhear that rant, it would have to be Trouble. I was so distracted by Katie that I didn't even hear the door chime.

I turned around to face Trouble, smoothing my apron and trying hard not to look like I was currently dying of embarrassment. "What can I get for you, Sam?"

"I'll have what you were having," he answered with a look of innocence.

"Very funny, Sam. Do you want an almond milk latte? If I remember correctly, you liked the one you had the other week."

Sam leaned over the counter as much as he could

without going completely over it. "Sure, I'll take that latte. But I would like to have something else as well."

"Oh, I have a new chocolate cupcake today. Would you like to try one of those with your coffee?" Maybe I could divert his mind out of his pants with chocolate? It was worth a try.

"Seriously, Evie. Please give me a chance. Let me take you out. I could personally promise that you would have... what did you call it? Oh, yes... 'mind-blowing,' 'bones melting,' 'fireworks' sex." He then ran a hand through his thick head of hair and gave me a dazzling smile.

From behind him, a hand shot out and grabbed his arm with enough force to spin him around. Ryan stood there, staring at Trouble with a look that would have struck fear into most men. But sadly, Trouble was not most men; this was Trouble in full hunting mode. Trouble just picked Ryan's hand off his arm.

"How does anything I am talking to Evie about somehow become any of your business?"

I have never understood the saying "spitting nails" when referring to a person being really angry. But after seeing the look on Ryan's face, I now knew exactly what that saying looked like.

"It becomes my business, PAL... when you are coming on to my girlfriend and making her obviously uncomfortable."

Trouble looked utterly shocked. "I am so sorry, man. I mean... I had no idea that Evie wasn't available."

Ryan gave him a look of distaste. "It shouldn't matter whether or not Evie was dating someone. When you see that you are making a lady feel uncomfortable, you move on. No one here wants to buy what you are selling. Now, take your latte and tip these ladies. And get on your way. You must be late for something?"

If Katie hadn't been there, I think I would have pulled Ryan around the counter and kissed him.

Ryan watched Trouble leave. "I'm sorry if I overstepped a bit there. I just saw him coming on to you —so over the top. Making you feel uncomfortable... and... I just saw red."

"Thank you, Ryan. Someone needed to stop him. And I don't personally care if he ever comes back. I don't need his latte business that bad."

That seemed to make Ryan feel better about the whole encounter. His usual smile returned to his face. "I was just stopping in for a cappuccino."

"And to see Evie. Of course." Katie smiled sweetly.

Ryan's voice dropped an octave. "And to see Evie," he confirmed.

I was finally able to tell Katie all about my weekend, and she couldn't have been happier. "Oh, I just knew there was an attraction there. I told you, didn't I?"

"Before you hurt yourself trying to pat yourself on the back, you have said that to me about a lot of men in the past. So many men that I think the odds were really stacked in your favour."

Instead of acknowledging what I'd just said, Katie simply skipped around behind the counter singing, "Evie's got a boyfriend, Evie's got a boyfriend."

I rolled my eyes. "I know, I know, first comes love, then comes marriage. I get it already."

Katie muttered to herself, just barely loud enough for me to hear. "Oh, you got it, alright."

SANDY ARRIVED at the end of the day for her usual pickup of my unsold baked goods. This time I was ready for; I grabbed the cardboard box of goodies and set it on the counter for her.

"Take a seat, Sandy. I kept back a cupcake for you, one I invented because of your brother's wedding. Well, your brother's wedding inspired it." I grabbed the last "Evie's Chocolate Fountain" cupcake from underneath the counter where I had stored it for her.

"You didn't have to do that, Evie. I'm glad you did, though." She looked the cupcake over and smiled. "I get it, the chocolate fountain, right?"

"Yes, I was inspired by that huge chocolate fountain they had at the reception. It was so decadent. I felt like a kid at Willy Wonka's Chocolate Factory. And afterwards, I felt kind of like an Oompa Loompa. I have never eaten that much chocolate at one time before. It's a surprise I didn't split the seams on my dress."

Sandy laughed at that. "I think everyone overindulged at that fountain. Who knew so many things can taste so much better when you cover them in chocolate?"

"Ding, ding, ding!" Katie cheered. "I'll take 'things that are obvious in life' for six hundred, Alex."

"Oh, you should have seen Evie's outfit at the

wedding, Katie. She was turning heads everywhere she went. I lost count of the number of times someone came up to me and asked who that beautiful lady was on my brother's arm."

"Stop it, Sandy, you're exaggerating. You should have seen Sandy's dress. It looked like it had been made with her in mind. That spring-green silk dress looked amazing on you. The way it draped, emphasized all your curves, and the silk shone under the lights."

"Thanks, Evie. I do love that dress. I am going to make an appointment with a seamstress to see about shortening it to a more cocktail length, so I can continue to wear it for special occasions."

I got my phone out and showed the pictures I had taken of the wedding party, so Katie could see how great Sandy looked in her dress.

"Oh, by the way. Before I forget, I wanted to tell you how much my mom enjoyed spending time with you. You know, she called me last night about you. I mean, that was the only reason she called. She just wanted to tell me how lovely you were with everyone. How much she enjoyed your company. She told me all about how you went to get my parents drinks and snacks when they were too busy catching up with long-distance family members to be eating and drinking as they should have. Oh, and she said, 'she has a lovely sense of humour too.'"

"That is so nice. Your mom and dad were just so sweet, and I felt really welcome. I'm going to thank them the very next time I see them."

. . .

AFTER SANDY HAD LEFT and we were locking up, Katie asked me who Sandy had brought as her plus one.

"No one. She came alone. And when I asked her if she had her date sitting all alone at one of the tables, she told me she wasn't dating anyone right now, and... how did she put it? 'I have no plans on dating anyone in the near future either.'"

Katie got that look on her face. The look that scares me, that look of stubborn resolve. "Good to know. Now that I have you successfully matched, I need a new challenge."

Poor Sandy. She is in for a wild ride and doesn't even know it yet.

Chapter Twenty-Five

The week after the wedding was filled with stolen hours and hurried passion. Ryan and I would meet at his house, sometimes in an early dash from work for both of us. Sometimes we would arrange to meet spontaneously after a text message from Ryan in the middle of the day, when he realized he suddenly had the chance to take an hour or so for himself. But no matter how we arranged these meetings, they seemed to happen every day, and they always ended the same way—falling into bed in a tangle of arms and legs, desperate to get each other's clothes off and lose ourselves in a world that contained just the two of us. There was never any hesitation on my part; when he called, I answered. I was like a horny teenager. The start of our sexual relationship seemed to open the floodgates for me and, in a way, make me almost shameless.

We never met at my house, always at Ryan's. For one thing, there were always Ryan's men working at my place, which would have been extremely awkward. For another, there was also Sara to think of. I was not ready to let things seem too serious, too fast. I figured that I would know when the time was right.

Although I was careful to keep my sex life with Ryan separate from the house, Sara seemed to know that something had changed with me, that it involved Ryan, and that it all started at the wedding.

"I DON'T KNOW how you do it," Sara said one evening while helping to clear the dishes from the table.

"How I do what?" I asked, puzzled.

"How you smile all day long and not get a sore face." She opened the freezer and proceeded to get herself a bowl of ice cream for dessert.

"You think I'm smiling more than usual?" I was trying for a casual tone.

"I know two things. One, that you are happier than I have seen you in years. And two, it is directly related to you dating Ryan."

"Sara, I..."

"Don't misunderstand me, Mom. This is a good thing. I am so happy for you, and happy for Ryan too. I mean, let's face it, the man is really punching above his weight in dating you."

"I just don't want you to get ahead of yourself, Sara. We are dating, and you're right, it's going really well. But it's still early days."

"Mom, I'm eighteen. I understand what dating is, and I have not skipped ahead in my mind to the two of you married and growing old together, don't worry. Although I think it's time you brought Ryan over here, maybe for dinner? I want to get to know the man making my mom smile all day long."

"Okay... That's fair. I will set something up for an evening next week." Sometimes when I look at Sara, I see a dramatic teenage girl, but other times I see an intelligent young lady. And that young lady is surprisingly insightful.

"And... drumroll, please. Speaking of making you smile... I have something to show you." She reached into her back pocket and unfolded a letter for me to read. It was an acceptance letter from one of the local universities.

"I am so happy for you!" I jumped up and ran around the table to hug her. "And so proud! So very proud."

"Thanks, Mom. It's only the first letter I've received; I am still waiting to hear back from the other two. But yes, I am thrilled. Do you know who else received an acceptance letter from this same university? Ann, but she got in for the Digital Arts program."

"Wow, that's great! Now you already know someone there."

"Speaking of that, I wanted to know if you were okay with me going with Ann this weekend to tour the school with her older cousin, who is in her first year and is staying in residence. We would stay over in sleeping bags on the floor of her cousin's dorm room and get a tour of the facilities and grounds. She said that we could even eat our meals in the cafeteria?"

"But if you went there, you wouldn't be in residence.

You wouldn't need to be. It's so close—you'd be living at home."

"I know that, Mom. It isn't about that. It's more about getting a real feel for the university itself. What amenities does it have? What is the atmosphere like? What is their cafeteria food like? Please, Mom! Ann and I are so excited. And you don't get an opportunity to look inside campus life every day."

"Sure, sweetie. That makes perfect sense. You and Ann will have a great time. Just ensure that this cousin doesn't drag you two to any wild parties."

"Of course. Thanks, Mom." Sara grabbed her phone and was already dialling Ann before she even left the table.

Friday morning I came back to the house for my regular coffee run/renovation catch-up with David and Paul. I was very impressed at how far along the basement had come. The drywall was up, and all the mudding and taping was complete; today, they said they would finish the ceiling with a smooth texture and then paint over that tomorrow.

"Once the ceiling is finished, we will start on plumbing work, like installing your shower, sinks, and toilet," Paul explained.

David came around the corner out of the soon-to-be complete bedroom. "Hey, Paul. Did you tell Mrs. Jones how great it is that she is dating the boss?"

Paul turned a few shades of pink and hissed, "No, David. That is their private business."

"Well, I know that. But... we were just talking about how great it is that you and Ryan are dating. He has been in such a great mood lately. He came by yesterday, and he was so happy with our progress that he gave us both a bonus. I have already spent mine, in my mind."

Paul looked embarrassed. "We weren't actually talking about you... it's just that we were talking about what a great mood he has been in lately. Since the two of you started dating. And I know it's none of our business." He now turned and gave David a dirty look. "It's just nice to see him happy. That's all."

It was really sweet how concerned they obviously were for Ryan. "Well, I think you both deserved that bonus. The basement is really coming together. Thanks." I only hope that was enough of a deflection from this awkward topic to stop any more discussion about my dating life.

"Thanks, Mrs. Jones. We're so glad that you like it so far." Paul beamed, and David nodded along in agreement.

Then as quick as my little legs could carry me, I disappeared upstairs.

THAT AFTERNOON I was back in the kitchen, going over the amount of money required for the new list of equipment and ingredients that Katie had supplied me with. I was still concerned about the number of additional sales I would need to make to cover these additional costs. On the other hand, I also knew that adding unique drinks to my menu could give me a decided edge. It might just bring some new customers to the café, customers who weren't getting the opportunity to try some of these more exotic drinks at their usual fast-food haunts. When I saw Katie had a minute and everyone in the café had been served, I pulled her over for a quick chat.

"Katie, I have gone over the equipment and ingredients cost for the new drinks that you would like to add to the menu. Even though I think I will probably lose money at the beginning, I think in the long run your ideas will bring more customers through the door. So, long story short, yes. I am going to take a chance on your ideas."

Katie squealed and did a cute little victory dance. "Thank you so much, Evie. You are not going to be sorry. I'm going to work really hard to make my new drinks a success."

Even though I knew this idea was taking a risk, it felt like I was actually taking that risk on Katie, and Katie was the type of friend worthy of that kind of trust.

WHEN I ARRIVED home after work, Sara was finishing packing her bags for her sleepover university experience, and she was almost giddy with excitement. I was still worried about the potential for problems, staying for the weekend at the university. But I knew this was really important to Sara, and she was right that it was a unique opportunity to see what campus life was like. I just made sure that she knew I was there to help her if she ran into any problems.

"I know that, Mom. I have my phone all charged up and packed my charger. I will send you texts and maybe even some pictures to let you know there aren't any problems."

I had agreed to let Sara take the car for the weekend, and I helped pack her backpack and sleeping bag into the trunk.

"Thanks again, Mom. I need to get to Ann's house. She just texted to say she is ready to go."

"Have fun and make good choices."

Sara simply rolled her eyes dramatically and waved as she backed down the driveway.

WITH SARA GONE, I packed an overnight bag for myself. Ryan was coming to pick me up for dinner at his house tonight, and I planned to make that dinner stretch over to include breakfast in bed.

Ryan helped me with my bag, putting it in the back of his truck for me. If he was surprised to see me bringing an overnight bag, he was careful not to show it.

After a delicious pasta dinner, he poured us both glasses of wine and motioned me toward the couch. I didn't need any encouragement to snuggle up and sip my wine.

"I have a dessert. Are you still full? We could have it a little later. Is that okay?"

"I couldn't eat another bite. But just out of curiosity, what did you make for dessert?"

"I didn't actually make anything. Diego—do you remember the owner of Naples' Son? He told me to get the best strawberries I could find, soak them in Prosecco, and then roll them in some sugar. And I was going to top that off with whipped cream."

"Sounds amazing."

"Can I ask you something?"

I nodded and took another sip of wine.

"The backpack you brought, does that mean what I think it means? Are you planning on staying the night?"

"I should have asked, I guess. But, yes, I was thinking of sleeping over if that's okay. You can say no if it doesn't work for you."

"Oh, I will definitely not say no to having you in my bed all night. How is this going to work with Sara?"

"Sara is away this weekend."

Ryan pulled me closer to him and whispered in my ear. "I know you've heard of breakfast in bed. But have you ever heard of dessert in bed?"

Chapter Twenty-Six

Ryan led me into his bedroom with my bag on one shoulder and a can of whipped cream in his other hand. As soon as he dropped my bag, he began to kiss me, warm and deep, while simultaneously unbuttoning my blouse. I returned the favour, and in quick order we were naked on the bed. Ryan grabbed the can of whipped cream from the bedside table where he had left it and gave me a wicked smile.

"Dessert time. Lie back for me."

I didn't need any more encouragement, and I settled myself on the top of his still-made bed. Still made? He's a single man who makes his bed! Men did that? Those thoughts went out the window though, because Ryan started applying the whipped cream to my nipples. Untangling such mysteries would have to wait.

I ended up with whipped-cream nipples and a long

arrow of cream that started between my breasts and ended with the point resting at my pubic hairline.

"What is that supposed to mean?" I asked as I lifted my head to look down at my body.

"I am going to follow the arrow... and see where it goes." He blinked and had a feigned look of innocence on his face.

"You mean like... this way to Evie's? Home of the world's best cherry tart?" I laughed and let my head rest once again on the bed.

"Yum. Cherry tart. You are making me hungry."

He then proceeded to lick and suck all the whipped cream from my nipples until they were pebbled and standing at attention. I began arching involuntarily towards him as he started the long, slow journey down toward the tip of the arrow. When he finally reached my pubic hairline, he looked up at me.

"I don't think I've ever had such a hankering for a cherry tart before." His warm hands spread my thighs apart, and he settled between them. His thumbs spread my folds, and he leaned forward and tasted me. I shuddered in response. Then he found just the perfect spot and sucked long and deep. I might have lost consciousness for a while because I was suddenly lying in a pool of sweat with his duvet gripped tightly in my fists. He suddenly lunged up my body, his arms holding his weight above me. I opened my eyes to see him staring intently at me.

"Evie," he said softly. "I think I'm falling in love with you."

"I think I'm falling in love with you too." It had just

slipped out of my mouth naturally, and I was pleased to realize that it was simply the truth. I put a hand against his chest, slowly but firmly pushed him back, and began to sit up.

"Sorry, Evie. I didn't mean to scare you. If things are moving too fast, we can slow things down. We can go at your own pace."

"You didn't scare me." I turned my head to look at him. "I do think I'm falling in love with you. And I'm not going anywhere. Well... anywhere except across the room to grab something out of my bag." I padded over to my overnight bag, which Ryan had left on a chair beside the large bay window.

As I unzipped the bag, I realized my hands were shaking.

Stop it! I scolded myself. *Get it together, Evie!* My nerves were getting the best of me. I could feel the bloom of a blush creeping across my cheeks, and my mouth was suddenly dry as dust. I grabbed a small black pouch out of the side pocket of my bag and walked tentatively back to Ryan.

"What's that?"

My hands shook as I undid the drawstring at the top of the pouch and very slowly pulled out a brand new, buttery soft latex toy. It had a handle, and at the other end there was a small round indent in the circular head. I held it out for Ryan to see, but I couldn't manage to make eye contact with him.

"It's my toy." I looked up briefly.

"Like a yo-yo?" He smiled goofily at me.

"What?" I was shocked—he seemed to be taking this

all so matter-of-factly. "It's an orgasm helper. Well... it's a vibrator." It was at that exact moment that I forced myself to make eye contact, and I am so glad that I did, because the look on his face was like a small child when he first sees all the presents Santa has left under the tree.

"I have never seen a vibrator like that before. I mean, aren't they usually... kind of... penis shaped?"

"This is a vibrator. I mean, the handle end still vibrates. But this end..." I pointed to the circular indent and suddenly I felt a giggle forcing its way up my throat. I don't know if it was just my nerves, or if the mental image of myself pointing out all the various features of my vibrator to my new boyfriend was causing me to feel like a model on *The Price Is Right*... for sex toys.

Come on, Evie! I forced myself to take a long, slow breath and focused on the task at hand. I pointed to the circular indent.

"This is where the magic happens. It creates suction, and when it is placed in just the right spot... instant orgasm. Well... almost instant."

"So, this mechanical suction feels good?"

"Amazing. There are times when I can get the 'big O' without too much trouble."

"Like a couple of minutes ago?" Cheeky smile.

"Yes, exactly like a few minutes ago." I playfully swatted his arm. My cheeks weren't feeling hot anymore, and I thought that I might have enough saliva now to be able to swallow. "There are also times, though, despite all kinds of work on John's part and me trying to will it into existence, it still just won't happen. In the end, I finally had to give up. And that feels incredibly frustrating. Not that I didn't still enjoy the sex, but... you know... I still felt like I had missed out on something. And I think that John did too."

I placed the vibrator gently on the bed between us. "I googled it. I looked up vibrators, and I found this one. Best purchase I have ever made."

"So, no more frustration?" His look had changed to one of open interest.

"No more frustration." I agreed. "Also, I can use it to be able to come during intercourse."

"You mean you can use it when I am inside you?"

"Yes, I was never able to orgasm during intercourse. Not without a little help. I learned that most women can't."

Ryan picked it up and looked it over intently. "What is it called?"

"I call it my 'Lady in Waiting.'"

Ryan laughed. "I get it. 'Her Highness' has a 'Lady in Waiting.' He began to push me back against the mattress gently. "You know they say you should try and learn something new every day?"

I raised my head off the bed. "I have heard that."

"Time to get me some more education."

SOME TIME LATER, I emerged from this lesson boneless and covered in sweat.

"Four times! I didn't even know that was possible. Imagine if I could come four times in a row."

I looked at him with one open eye. "You would probably be the human equivalent of a raisin."

We laughed together, and he laid on the mattress along my side. He cradled my jaw, and I turned my head towards him. "So how exactly do we use the 'Lady in Waiting' while I am inside you? It just looks too bulky to fit between us in the missionary position. And it would never stay put with you bouncing on top."

"Here, I'll show you." I grabbed all the pillows from his bed. And because he is a man, that meant two, not six, like on my bed. I piled them on top of each other about one foot from the edge of the bed. I then proceeded to place my knees near the edge of the bed, and with my tummy supported by the pillows, I lay across them. I rested one arm straight above my head and then reached my other arm around the pillows with the vibrator, and I placed it in just the right spot. I eased my bum back out over the edge of the bed and turned the vibrator on. I waited a few moments, but Ryan hadn't moved behind me. I raised myself up on my arm enough to turn around and look back at him. He was standing there, completely still. His gaze was dark and full of hunger.

"Is everything okay?"

After a beat of silence, he answered. "That is the single most erotic sight I have ever seen."

"Oh... okay. Well then... I guess... enjoy the view." I smiled to myself as I slowly turned back around and settled in once more.

He still didn't move for a few minutes more, and by that time, the vibrator had begun to work its magic. He watched me as I fell apart. Then his large, warm hands softly but firmly grabbed my hips. His impossibly heated chest was against my back as he leaned forward to kiss my neck.

"You are the most desirable woman. I can't remember ever feeling so excited."

I smiled against the mattress, and he entered me in one smooth, fluid motion. We rocked together until I came with a lingering pulsing that pushed him over the edge as well.

AFTER BEING TANGLED in each other's arms, I turned towards him to find him lying on his back with his arm over his forehead, staring up at the ceiling.

"We had a good sex life. I mean Deb and me. But... Deb would not have been open to adding toys in the bedroom. And doggy style... well, it seemed to make her feel uncomfortable. Maybe she felt too vulnerable and spread out like that. We tried it a few times, but I could feel her hesitation. So I didn't push it. But you... tonight, all splayed out in front of me with your toy. It was something to see. And the sex felt like pure joy, pure pleasure. It's a memory I'll replay in my mind... probably until the day I die."

THE FOLLOWING day I woke to an empty bed. I reached my leg over and Ryan's side still felt warm, so I knew he hadn't been gone long. I snuggled under his fluffy duvet and contemplated trying to go back to sleep again when he came through the doorway with two mugs of coffee.

Lisa Plaice

"Good morning." He set a mug down for me on the bedside table and leaned in for a kiss.

"Good morning to you. Coffee delivered right to my bedside. Now that's a good morning."

"I figured, you deliver coffee in the morning to the masses. It was high time someone returned the favour."

We sat up in bed, drinking our coffee and just generally enjoying each other's company. I grabbed my phone and quickly checked in with Sara. Apparently, they were having a great time, and she had recently finished having breakfast in the cafeteria with Ann and her cousin. The eggs were gross, she said, but everything else was pretty tasty. They were just about to start their tour at the campus library, so I let her go.

"What do you think about going out to breakfast?" Ryan asked. "I'm not that great at breakfast, and I know one thing for sure, bacon always tastes better if I don't have to cook it or clean up afterwards."

"Sounds good to me."

Chapter Twenty-Seven

I arrived back on Sunday afternoon, making it home before Sara. My weekend with Ryan had gone by too fast. We cooked for each other with the food we bought at the farmers' market. Saturday night, we enjoyed a big bonfire in his backyard, with the two of us snuggled up on one of his cushioned oversized loungers. Beneath a large quilt Ryan brought out, we made love under the light of the stars and the flickering flames.

My feelings for Ryan were becoming stronger by the day, and I could tell he felt the same. When I was with him, I felt happy and alive in a way that I hadn't in years. Katie had been bugging me for two years now to take a chance. How often has she told me that love is a chance worth taking? Well, I have taken a chance on Ryan, a huge chance. And for once, I was going to try and take each day as it came. Oh, and maybe not overthink everything.

. . .

KATIE REMINDED me later that same week that we hadn't been out to karaoke in a long time.

"The kids are great, Evie. You know I think my kids are great. But if I don't get away from them for a night, really soon. I might go insane."

"You? Insane? I am trying to picture that. How exactly would that look any different from... oh, today, for example?"

"Ha, Ha. Very funny. Now, are we going to karaoke Friday night or what?"

"Friday night at Archie's, try to stop me."

"That's the spirit."

BETH STOPPED into the café on Wednesday afternoon, and she looked like she was in desperate need of some caffeine.

"A cappuccino with a double shot of espresso and extra foam, please."

"Coming up. How is your dad doing, by the way? Is he still grumpy about the diet?"

"Oh, he's a little better at eating my cooking. Don't get me wrong. He still misses his butter and red meat and beer. And coffee, you know... real coffee. But at least he eats more now and grumbles a little less."

"Why don't I make him a decaffeinated cappuccino to go for you to take home? First things first, though. Let's have a little catch-up while you have your drink."

I directed Beth to a corner table that had a bit more privacy. I took my break, and we updated each other on what was new in our lives. Beth still had a little vacation time left, but she was worried about how she would manage to juggle remote working from Haven.

"A large portion of my job can be done remotely. There's also, however, some necessary travel overseas coming up. So I can attend trade fairs and visit my main suppliers, to preorder from their samples and gauge upcoming trends."

"Oh, I thought they would have your assistant do the overseas work for you while you are working from your dad's."

"No, they can't send my assistant. In my job, most of the actual purchasing is made through my strong working relationships with the suppliers. I think that, sooner rather than later, I'll have to start looking into hiring a nurse who can stay with Dad when I have to be away."

"I will help you any way that I can. Although I am limited to times outside the café hours. Hey, speaking of nurses, do you remember Aiden from high school?"

"Aiden? How could I forget him? He was my first crush."

"Did you know that Aiden changed careers a few years ago? He went back to school and got his nursing degree. Last I heard, he was working for a short-term nursing agency. I can give you the agency's phone number."

"Thanks, that would be a perfect place to start."

Beth told me how she was slowly getting used to being back in a small town again. After so many years of being in the city, she found some of our small-town idiosyncrasies annoying. Like how she finds that, no matter what, she always runs into someone she knows at the store. And she always seems to have something embarrassing in her hand, like tampons or laxatives. She told me about one particular time when a family friend had her penned into a corner at the grocery store, asking her all sorts of personal health questions about her dad. Questions that she didn't feel comfortable answering. In the end, she said she had just looked at her watch and made up an important doctor's appointment. She gently but firmly told her that she would be late if she didn't leave right away.

"By the way, what the hell is with the hours the stores in this town keep? If I needed a carton of milk in the city at two in the morning, no problem. Here in Haven, you can't even get gas after midnight!"

"Funny, I guess I'm just so used to the shorter hours here. I don't even think about it."

"How do you stand having no privacy? I have had not one, not two, but three busybodies come up to me to ask about my divorce."

"I hope you told them to mind their own business."

"No, even better. I told them that Chris was a closet clown... then I went into great detail about how he got off on having sex while fully dressed as a clown. Big curly wig, oversized shoes, red nose that honks, and everything."

"Oh my God, how I have missed you, Beth! If only I could have been a fly on the wall for those conversations."

. . .

I HAD ASKED Ryan to join Sara and me for dinner that evening. I was looking forward to seeing Sara and Ryan get to know each other better. Luckily, I hadn't started making dinner yet when Ryan called me to cancel.

"Evie, I know this is really short notice. I am so sorry, but... could we possibly move tonight's dinner to tomorrow?"

"Emergency at work?"

"No, an emergency call from a friend."

"Oh, I hope there is nothing seriously wrong."

"I think that copious amounts of alcohol are involved. So, I am going to go over and see if there is anything I can do. I feel terrible about this, though. Leaving you and Sara in the lurch like this."

"Don't worry about it. I hadn't even started supper yet."

"Good. Tomorrow night, you, Sara, and I should go to that great Thai restaurant you took me to, my treat."

"Oh, that's actually not going to work. Sara has a long shift at the drugstore tomorrow night. She starts right after school, and she works till closing."

"Well, just you tomorrow night then? And Sara can pick any restaurant she wants for another night that works better for her."

"You don't have to do that. But I know that Sara would love it. Beware though. She has expensive tastes."

"Not a problem. Are you free tomorrow night for some Thai food and my company? Let's say six o'clock. I will pick you up at a quarter to six at your place."

"Alright. Sounds yummy."

"Please say sorry to Sara. She can pick her favourite

spot or a restaurant she has always wanted to try. I really do feel bad about this. But... I got this phone call... and..."

"Go. Don't worry about it. Sara will understand. I will see you tomorrow. I hope everything is okay with your friend."

"Thanks for understanding."

Sara was great about the whole thing. She seemed excited to pick any restaurant she wanted, and just as I predicted, she wanted to go to the local fancy-schmancy steak house.

"At least we know he's a great friend, right? But don't think it didn't escape my notice that you are getting two dinners out of this, and I'm only getting one. So... maybe you could bring me home a side order of their crispy spring rolls?"

"Cheeky! I will see what I can do."

"I was going to surprise you at dinner... but... ta-da!" With a flourish, she presented me with a folded piece of paper.

"Another acceptance letter! Congratulations! You now have your pick of both local universities. That's awesome."

"Thanks, Mom. I'm not going to lie, it feels great."

"Has Olivia heard from any universities yet?"

"No, not yet. She only applied to the University of British Columbia, and just like me, she hasn't heard one way or the other."

"Only applying to one university? I wonder why she did that."

"She told me that she either wanted to go there or

nowhere at all. That's Olivia, though. I love her, but... she is kind of dramatic."

"Well, I am proud of you. Your dad would have been so proud."

"Thanks, Mom. I know he would have been. He would be telling everyone he met, wouldn't he?"

"He would already be on the phone boasting to your grandma and grandpa."

"Speaking of which..." I said as I fumbled for my phone on the kitchen counter, "I am going to call your grandparents right now and tell them the good news."

Chapter Twenty-Eight

I found myself struggling to get my red cashmere sweater over my head without ruining my carefully curled hair. Once I got my arms through the sleeves, my wristwatch caught my eye, and I realized I was now running late. With Ryan's consistent punctuality, I knew he would already be waiting in the driveway. So I threw on my high-heeled ankle boots and clumped my way down the stairs.

"Sorry, I'm late," I said as Ryan opened my door, and I leaned forward to kiss him hello. Ryan kissed me back, but when he pulled away, I saw some sadness in his eyes.

"Is everything okay?" I asked him as he backed down the driveway.

"Yes, everything is fine. Why?"

"You just look kind of down."

"Probably just tired. I had a hell of a day today. Everything that could go wrong did."

The rest of the ride consisted of Ryan telling me

about the various things that had gone wrong on a couple of his job sites. Including running into an unexpected wiring nightmare at a Victorian house he was currently renovating for a very picky couple. Apparently they were unamused and seemed unable to grasp that this setback meant more money would be required of them. That and the fact that the expected finish date was going to have to be pushed out. Otherwise, it was a barrage of broken equipment, missing tiles that had been specially ordered, and men off sick.

I put my hand on his thigh and squeezed. "That sounds like a stressful day. Let's go in and enjoy a relaxing dinner and try not to think about it for a while."

Ryan smiled and squeezed my hand. When he did, I noticed that his smile seemed a little forced. The corners of his eyes didn't crinkle up like they usually did. I decided to keep the conversation light tonight and try to get his mind off his stressful day.

THE MEAL WAS JUST as delicious as last time, and we ended up ordering the same entrees, just with different meat choices. We switched up the appetizers, though, and I remembered to put in Sara's spring roll order to go.

Ryan still seemed distracted, but my funny stories involving Katie and I started bringing him out of his shell. He had just excused himself to go and use the restroom when I remembered that I had never asked him about what had happened with his friend last night. Almost immediately after he left the table, his cell phone pinged with an incoming text. His phone had been left on the table, sitting sideways, closer to my side of the table than his, and the text was in bold letters across the top of the screen.

> Thank you so much for last night. I was hoping to see you again tonight. Can you drop by later?

What the hell? The name of the sender was Lena. Lena was the friend he went to help last night? Drop by later? Okay, Evie... take a breath. I was trying not to jump to any conclusions. Lena has been a friend of his for years; this is nothing strange. Another ping sounded.

> That kiss was a surprise. But a good surprise.

It felt like all the air had suddenly been sucked out of the room. Kiss? They had kissed last night? I had specifically asked him about Lena after that evening, playing pool at Archie's. He said they were just friends. I suddenly had the urge to throw up. I grabbed my phone and called for an Uber. Then I fished some money out of my wallet and placed it under my glass. I had already grabbed my purse and had just finished putting my coat on when Ryan returned to the table.

"What's the matter? Where are you going?"

"It's my friend, Beth." I lied. My mind was still spinning. "She is on her way to pick me up. She needs some help with her dad."

"Beth should stay at home with her dad. I'll drive you over, and then maybe I can help too." Ryan started to try and wave the waitress over for the cheque.

"Thanks for the offer. But she will almost be here by now. You've had a long day, don't worry. It isn't anything the two of us can't handle ourselves."

The confusion on Ryan's face was hard to look at, and I could feel the pricking of tears starting to form in my eyes. I gave him my best attempt at a sunny smile, and I looked down at my phone as it suddenly vibrated.

"Oh, she's here in the parking lot. I have to go."

Ryan reached over to kiss me and ended up grazing my cheek as I scrambled to leave.

"Okay... If you're sure I can't help . . . call me if that changes. I could come right over if you need me."

Just like you helped Lena last night? I wondered.

As I opened the restaurant door to meet the Uber driver parked out front, I could barely hear Ryan call after me.

"You forgot about Sara's spring rolls."

I didn't acknowledge him or turn around because the tears had already started to fall.

IF THE UBER driver was surprised by an openly crying middle-aged lady getting into the back of his car, he was careful not to show it. I am not sure why, but I gave him Katie's address instead of my own. I second-guessed that decision when we pulled up outside her house to find all the windows dark.

"Can you just stay here and wait for me while I make sure my friend is home?" He nodded in agreement. But my fears were unfounded as Katie answered the door after the first knock, and I was immediately enveloped in a big bear hug and almost pulled in the door after she took one look at my tear-stained face. I turned and waved the Uber driver off and then immediately dropped my purse and coat in the front hall.

Katie found me minutes later sprawled across the living room couch with my arm over my eyes.

"Here, get this down your throat." She handed me a glass of white wine. "Now, what in the hell has happened? Didn't you and Ryan have a dinner date tonight?"

I sat up partway on the couch to take a sip of wine without spilling the glass down my front.

"Don't worry about Mark or the kids, by the way." Katie offered me a Kleenex from a box that had been sitting on the coffee table in front of me. "The kids are already in bed. Poor Mark had a bad migraine, and as soon as his painkillers kicked in, he was fast asleep."

I blew my nose a little louder than I meant to. And I gave Katie an apologetic grimace. "Thanks, Katie. I'm not sure why I came. I mean... I know why I came... but... I didn't plan to just drop in on you like this. But... without thinking about it... I just gave the Uber driver your address. Sorry." I was now slumped over the side of the couch, resting my weary head on the armrest.

"No apology is necessary. You are obviously upset. Now, please tell me what's wrong."

I raised my head off the armrest with great effort to take another sip—well, a big gulp, if I'm being honest. "Ryan and I were having dinner at the Thai restaurant."

Katie made a twirling motion with her hand as if to say get the hell on with the story.

"He seemed a little distracted tonight, sad or tired. And he said that it was just a really bad day." I took a deep breath and steeled myself for the rest of the story. "Anyway, we were just talking like normal and then at the end of the meal, he excused himself to go and use the restroom."

"He didn't go out the back door instead and stiff you with the cheque?!" Katie had a horrified look on her face.

"No. Why would you guess that?"

"Because you're taking too long to tell me what happened, and my mind is literally spinning out with all the possibilities."

"He cheated," I said very quietly and with great effort. I placed my head back against the armrest.

"I must have heard that wrong. He cheated? How do you know for sure? He told you that?" The edge creeping into Katie's voice was the only warning usually given before she completely lost it.

"I saw the text."

"What text? From who?"

"Ryan's phone was kind of turned away from him a little. So, when he went to the bathroom, and the text came in, I could read it perfectly."

Katie glared at me like she might hurt me if I didn't hurry up and spill all the details.

"It was from Lena. She said '*thanks for that kiss, it was unexpected* and *are you going to drop by tonight.*'" It all came spilling out at once.

"What? He went and saw Lena last night? Lena was the friend 'in need' that he had to cancel on you and Sara for?"

I simply nodded. No words necessary.

"I will kill him!" The look flashing in her eyes told me that, given the opportunity, she would.

"Don't yell. You'll wake Mark and the kids."

"Bastard." That came out as an angry whisper. "He told you he wasn't interested in Lena. That she was 'just a friend.'" She used exaggerated air quotes.

"Well, I guess he lied. Or... he changed his mind."

"What did he say when you confronted him?"

"I didn't confront him. I think I was in shock. I made up an excuse that I had to go and help Beth with her dad. I had already called an Uber, and I just left." At that exact moment, my phone chimed with its incoming text sound from the coffee table, where I had thrown it after fishing it out of my pocket. It was from Ryan.

Please call me.

Katie leaned down to read the text. "Text him back and blast him. What is the appropriate emoji for a 'rat bastard asshole'? A man on a toilet, followed by a rat, followed by the devil?" she pondered. I turned my phone off and laid back down on the couch.

"It's my fault, really."

"What? Seriously. What kind of nonsense is that?"

"Not that he cheated. No, the fact that it hurts so much. I let myself fall for him even though I knew he was too young for me. He probably wants to have a relationship with Lena because it could end in a marriage with kids of his own and no baggage to carry around. I mean, here I am, a widow, having already had my family. I knew that he would want to have kids. I mean, that's what ultimately caused his divorce. Well, that and Deb cheating, but I think it all started with wanting kids." I now felt exhausted by the conversation.

"Everybody has baggage. Don't kid yourself—everybody. At least yours is cute, and it matches."

Katie was trying to get me to laugh, but it wasn't working.

"If Ryan cheated, it's because he is a scumbag. And Ryan being a scumbag, that's a pre-existing condition and has nothing to do with you. Or having kids or being a widow." Katie had crouched down, so her face was almost in line with mine. "You deserve to be loved by someone who not only loves your baggage but is also willing to help you unpack it." She squeezed my arm. "I am here for you and on your side, always. What do you need right now, at this moment?"

"I think I need a ride back home to my car so I can drive and pick up Sara after her shift finishes." I looked at my watch. "Which is in fifteen minutes."

"I will do you one better. I am going to run you home and drop you off. Then I will pick Sara up and drop her off at home. I'll tell her you have a bad headache and that you've gone to bed. And it's not a lie because, after all that crying, I'm sure you really do have a headache."

I nodded slowly and carefully, stood up, and crammed my phone back into my back pocket while it chimed and vibrated with another incoming text message.

. . .

BACK IN MY ROOM, all snuggled under my duvet, I heard another text coming in on my phone lying beside me on my bedside table.

Evie?

What's going on?

At least let me know that you're okay.

I knew the texts weren't going to stop. I typed a simple reply.

Home safe and sound.

Then I powered my phone off and cried myself to sleep.

Chapter Twenty-Nine

The next morning, I shuffled to the bathroom and looked at myself in the mirror. My eyes were terribly swollen from all the crying the night before. I looked like a train wreck. Maybe I should go into the café and do the morning baking, then head back home and hide under the covers? I decided to try a second option, at least for another thirty minutes, by lying back down in bed with some cold cucumber slices on my eyelids.

Thirty minutes later I examined my eyes and found that I looked like I could maybe pass as having had a bad allergic reaction to... what? To dust? Yeah, that should work. I will tell anyone bold enough to ask that I had a bad allergic reaction from tackling an intense spring cleaning last night. In truth, I had experienced a bad reaction to Ryan blowing off a dinner date in order to secretly meet up with Lena and what? Make out? What kind of kiss did they share, exactly? Closed-mouth?

Open-mouth? French? Probably French, with lots of tongue and soft sighing. I thought about the two of them kissing and it kept coming back into my mind unwanted, the same way your tongue finds a sore tooth repeatedly. I wonder why we do that to ourselves. Is it a question that we feel compelled to ask repeatedly? Does it still hurt? Let's think about it some more... imagine it happening again... maybe it doesn't hurt anymore... nope, that's confirmed. It still hurts.

THE MORNING RUSH WAS OVER, and Katie and I finally had time to restock and have a coffee break. Katie was being extra funny today; I mean, she made up a dirty limerick right on the spot. I knew she was doing her best to try and keep me distracted. Between the baking, the morning rush, and Katie's craziness, I was managing not to mentally probe my sore tooth too much. But then something caught my eye: Ryan's blue work truck was currently pulling up to park across the street.

"I am not here. I have gone out on a supply run." I grabbed my coffee and headed as quickly as my feet would carry me to the safety of the kitchen.

A few minutes later, Katie popped her head in the kitchen door. "The coast is clear."

"I'm sorry for making you deal with Ryan. I just can't handle it yet."

"Not a problem. It's totally understandable. Anyone that would cheat on you is a fool, and I don't suffer fools."

"What did he want? I mean, what did he say?"

"He asked for you, and I told him he had just missed you."

"Well, that was true."

"He said he had been trying to get hold of you, but you haven't been answering your phone. He said you left the restaurant suddenly last night and that he's worried about you. He asked me if I would 'please ask Evie to give me a call tonight.' He seemed really worried about you. I have never seen him without a bright smile, and he didn't even want a coffee. he came to the café specifically to talk to you."

"Again, I'm sorry if I put you in a difficult position. It feels stupid to me to be so upset about Ryan cheating on me. I mean, after losing John... how could this... relationship? Hurt so much? I feel stupid. I opened my heart to him. I took a chance. I should have known better."

"No problem. Don't kill the messenger, but... is it possible that you misinterpreted those texts? He just seemed so genuinely upset and worried about you."

"He told me he couldn't make dinner with Sara and me because he had to help a 'friend in need.' And that same friend is wondering if he is stopping by her place after our date. Oh, and she wants to talk about the kiss they had shared. How could all that be innocent? I mean, you should have seen the way she was staring at him all night at Archie's. She was mooning over him, really. Obviously, she was in love with him, and I asked Ryan. I point-blank asked him if he wanted to ask her out." I had officially run out of steam and energy. I rested my head on the counter because, suddenly, my neck no longer had the strength to hold it up.

"Never mind." Katie massaged the side of my neck with one hand. "I love you. And I am team Evie all the way; you know that." She then proceeded to mime cheering my name with her imaginary pom-poms.

THAT NIGHT AFTER WORK, I decided to drive home purposely by The Penthouses. I slowed and then stopped in front of the billboard when I saw that the banner across it seemed to have changed. It now read "Sold Out." Sold out? Sold out!? When did that happen? Where was I? Oh yes, now I remember where I was. I was googly-eyed over Ryan. I was in a bubble. A bubble of lust, thinking about him, having sex with him at all hours of the day. Damn it! I took my eye off the ball! How could I have been so stupid? I punched the top of the dashboard with both hands. Ouch, that actually hurts. I am going to take some time out of my day tomorrow and come down for a talk with the management here. Is it possible that someone is on the fence? Maybe, just maybe, someone was about to pull out. *Tomorrow,* I confirmed that thought in my mind. *Tomorrow I will try and undo this damage that I allowed to happen while I had my eye off the ball and on Ryan.*

I HADN'T RETURNED to the house for my usual morning meeting with David and Paul. I couldn't take the chance that Ryan might be there. But imagining them waiting patiently for their daily coffees made me feel terrible. It wasn't their fault that their boss was a cheater. I texted Paul and told him that I was just too busy with the café to bring them their usual coffee. But if they wanted to swing by the café on their way to work, I would ensure that they continued to receive their daily caffeine hit on me.

TEXTS FROM RYAN kept coming in.

> Call me please; I need to know you're okay.

> I think there has been some kind of misunderstanding. I'm going to stop by your place tonight.

But I ignored the texts, and when my doorbell rang that night, for once I seemed to have caught a break, as Sara was out at work. I wouldn't have wanted my daughter to see her strong, independent mother hiding in the house, careful to stay away from the windows so that Ryan couldn't know I was home. Luckily, I was hiding in the kitchen pantry because he called my cell phone as soon as he stopped ringing the doorbell. I had the ringer on high, and I knew that being in the pantry with the door shut, he couldn't have possibly heard my cell phone ringing inside the supposedly empty house.

. . .

WHEN SARA RETURNED FROM WORK, I was already in bed with the lights off. She knocked softly at the door and then slowly opened it a crack.

"Mom? Are you okay? Is something wrong?"

"Nothing's wrong. I'm just tired, really tired. It's been a long couple of days, and I'm down on my sleep."

"Okay." Silence for a beat. "Get a good night's sleep. Love you." And then the door slowly and quietly shut until I heard a soft click and the sound of footsteps retreating down the hall.

MY MEETING the next morning with the manager of The Penthouses did not go well. According to him, not only were all the condo units sold out, but there was also a waiting list. A *long* waiting list for any units that, for some unforeseen reason, had come back on the market. But, he told me with a smile, it wasn't all bad news. He said I could put my name down for a unit in their eventual phase two building complex. When I asked him when that was expected to start, I was devastated to learn that he estimated phase two to be completed in approximately two years' time. Two years? This is what I get for letting myself fall so completely for Ryan!

Chapter Thirty

My problems with sleep ramped up after breaking up with Ryan. I still managed to make it into the café for the early morning baking. But I hadn't yet been able to last through the whole day at the café. I was lucky to have Katie able to close up for me because, in the afternoon, I would ultimately run out of energy and need to go home to bed. Katie had taken over the job of wrapping up the day-olds and handing them over to Sandy. Katie told me that Sandy always looked expectantly around for me when she arrived, but outside of asking how I was doing, she never mentioned Ryan.

PAUL AND DAVID showed up just after opening a few days later for their offered caffeine fix. After placing their coffee orders, Paul leaned on the counter and asked if he could talk to me privately for a minute. Katie overheard the request and nodded me away with her head and a serious look on her face.

"You haven't been by the basement for a while now, and I just wanted to give you a few updates."

"Of course. I've been checking on your progress regularly, and it looks amazing."

"Yes, it does, doesn't it?" Paul gave me a hesitant smile. "I wanted to let you know that we are all finished with the kitchen and bathroom countertops, and in the next few days, we are hoping to start installing the fireplace."

"Oh, that sounds great. I can't wait to see the fireplace in; it's going to look amazing."

There was a beat of silence.

"I'm just going to go ahead and ask." David shot a sideways glance at Paul. "I know that it's none of my business. I mean, I know that you and Ryan aren't dating anymore... and... I don't know why. But... you should know that Ryan is miserable. Whatever happened? I just wanted you to know that Ryan has been showing up every day, and it's obvious he is only showing up to try and run into you."

"David, I know you're telling me this because you just want Ryan and me to be happy. But it really is a private issue."

Paul gave David an "I told you so" kind of look.

"I'm sorry if I overstepped. It really isn't any of my business."

"You're right. It isn't." But saying that made me feel like crap when I saw David and Paul's faces fall. "Thank you for caring, though."

. . .

AFTER THAT UNCOMFORTABLE CONVERSATION, the rest of the day seemed more manageable in comparison. I was surprised to find that I'd actually made it through the day. Sandy breezed through the door and stopped just inside it when she saw me behind the counter.

"How are you?" she asked gently when she arrived at the counter. She asked it in the same way you ask an elderly aunt you are visiting in the hospital, right after she fell and broke her hip. You know the answer, you know that she is in a lot of pain, but you have to ask anyway.

"I am doing okay." I tried to appear all casual and failed. I knew she could see through my terrible acting job.

"Ryan hasn't told me what happened. He tends to keep this type of thing to himself. I do know that the two of you aren't seeing each other anymore. And I will shut up on the subject afterwards, but I have to get this one thing out. Whatever happened, you should know that Ryan really cared about you and that he would never do anything to hurt you."

Huh. Really? So he unintentionally kissed Lena, and his passion for her overtook him? But none of that had anything to do with Sandy. And I was hoping to get through this with my friendship with Sandy somewhat intact.

"Sometimes things just don't work out." I tried that casual look thing again. Maybe practice makes perfect? If

Sandy saw through it this time, then she was a better actress than me because I couldn't tell.

"I won't say any more on the subject. My lips are sealed." Then she pretended to zip her lips shut.

KATIE REMINDED me about our failed karaoke night when I was locking up.

"We missed our karaoke night at Archie's last Friday night. And I know you probably still don't feel like going out. But I think it would do you good to get out and get your mind off things."

I was just about to say no. My lips were already forming the word when suddenly, nothing would come out. Having a few margaritas at Archie's and singing my heart out suddenly seemed like the perfect evening.

"Let's go. Meet you there at eight."

"Wow. You said yes. Okay, I will meet you at Archie's at eight tonight. Now I am going to run away with my fingers in my ears and my cell phone turned off, so you can't change your mind."

Sassy, and I couldn't argue with her.

I ARRIVED at Archie's in an Uber, after having a few glasses of wine while getting dressed, continually trying to talk myself into this evening out. I walked in the door with my head held high. I had my coolest-looking high-heeled black leather boots on. The silver rivets and the oversized buckle gave them some decided edge. I matched them to my black leather jacket. I would have looked like a motorcycle gang wanna-be, except I totally redeemed the look with a bright orange silk blouse and a pair of dark blue jeans. My hair was curled and my makeup was flawless, so even though I felt crushed deep inside, I knew I looked my best. And looking my best might be the only armour I had at the moment. It would have to do.

Katie was waiting for me upstairs in the karaoke room with two lime margaritas already lined up for me. You have got to love Katie; everyone needs a Katie in their life. Four margaritas and a basket of wings later, Katie and I were poring over the song menu. Our routine was that we both had to pick two songs to sing on our own, and we would pick one song together that we would sing as a duet.

Katie dabbed the last of the barbecue sauce off her mouth with a napkin. "That's you—they just called your name. See you on the other side. Break a leg and all that. Scratch that. I shouldn't have said that. Your heels are too high. Break a sweat, maybe?"

I had chosen to sing the song *Jolene*, by Dolly Parton. I felt like belting out that song in particular would be kind of cathartic. I became the song more than I just sang it; I felt it and lived through it. When the song ended, I found myself standing on the stage with tears rolling down my cheeks and everyone in the audience on their feet, clapping and cheering for me. When I made my way through the crowd, Katie was standing at our table, waiting to give me a big bear hug. With her mouth near my ear, she whispered, "He was here, you know." I pulled away from her to look wildly around the bar.

"What? You mean Ryan?"

"Who else? Yes, Ryan. He was sitting at that corner table way over there." She pointed over to the far corner table that now sat empty. And then I remembered: this was Ryan's pool night. Damn it! How could I have forgotten that this was Ryan's pool night? Katie grabbed my face with both hands and forced me to maintain eye contact with her.

"Listen to me. He arrived just after you took the stage, and he sat alone. He couldn't take his eyes off you. He waited until the song ended, and then he snuck out that side door."

"He has a regular game of pool here tonight with his friends. Crap! How could I have forgotten that? How the hell am I going to get out the front door of Archie's without running into him snuggling up to Lena?" I felt panicky and damp with sweat.

"Listen to me. Are you listening to me? You have that deer in the headlights look that usually means your mind is spinning out of control, and you are no longer able to listen to anything or anyone else around you."

I made eye contact again and tried my best to focus on what Katie was saying.

"We are going to finish with our duet as planned, and you are going to order a coffee while we wait for our turn. Then you are going to use caffeine to try and get some more focus back. When the duet is over, you are going to wait for me here at the table."

"But where will you be?"

"I will be downstairs scoping out Ryan and his friends' whereabouts. Who knows? They may have left the bar by that time. And if they haven't, I will make sure to wait until they are really engrossed in their game, and then I will text you to make your exit quickly."

"Thanks, Katie." I was almost blubbering with relief. "I owe you."

"Don't even think about it. If the roles were reversed, you would do the same thing for me."

IT WAS the single most awkward duet in history. I couldn't concentrate on the words. I was too busy trying to see if Ryan had returned. But all the bright stage lights made that impossible. As we made our way back to the table, I could see my coffee had arrived while we were singing, and I took a big gulp.

"Remember, keep the volume on your phone up and have it vibrate as well. That way, you won't miss my text." And with that, Katie grabbed her enormous bag, slung her jean jacket across her shoulders, and disappeared down the steps.

I had almost finished my coffee when her texts came in.

> Come down now. Coast is clear.

I didn't even try to sneak a peek at the pool tables when I got down to the main floor. I just beelined it straight for the front door. Once outside, I leaned against the brick wall and tried to catch my breath. Katie came out the door after me, and she waited beside me until the wheezing had stopped. Maybe I should seriously think about a gym membership.

We had decided to walk to Katie's house because she only lived a few blocks away. Then I would order an Uber from there to take me the rest of the way home.

"She wasn't there. Lena, I mean. She wasn't playing pool with Ryan tonight. It was a group of four men. Ryan and two of his friends seemed to be waiting for the third man to come back with their drink order. So I just waited by the bar until they all had their drinks and they were back into their game again."

"Thanks, Katie—you're a lifesaver."

"Have you spoken to Ryan? Or returned any of his text messages?"

"No, not yet. I am waiting to speak to him. I will call him when I know I can do it without crying. I get it—Ryan gets to change his mind and date someone else. The way he did it was nasty, and definitely not okay. But I don't want to make him feel guilty for no longer wanting to date me or embarrass myself by blubbering all over him."

"Team Evie. All the way."

"Please, don't start with that cheer again. I don't think I can take anyone being too nice to me right now. I think it might make me start to cry."

Katie put one hand into her enormous purse and pulled out a small travel container of tissues.

"Cry away."

Chapter Thirty-One

The next morning when I finally peeled myself out of bed and down the stairs, I found Sara waiting for me at the kitchen table, drinking a cup of coffee.

"Oh, you have read my mind," I said as I poured myself a cup and then proceeded to cradle the mug like a tiny baby. "You have no idea how badly I needed this."

"Come and sit with me." Sara pulled out the chair next to her at the table. "I have some exciting news." She seemed to be vibrating.

"Okay, what's so exciting?" I asked as I sank slowly into the chair beside her, waiting for my thumping headache to settle down after that movement. I wasn't sure how much excitement I could take at this very moment, but I certainly didn't want to dampen Sara's good mood.

"I got in!" Sara was waving a letter in the air, in front of my face. "I got into the University of British Columbia!

Can you believe it? There is sooo much competition for their Psychology program. I hoped, but I never really thought that I had a chance." She now stood up from her chair and began a twirling kind of dance around the table. "I got in and Olivia got in as well. Different programs, but on the same campus. I mean, what are the odds? Now we can both go together and not feel lonely or awkward because we'll have each other. I got in!"

I felt all the blood leave my face and the room started to spin slightly—this time it was *not* the effects of my hangover. What was happening here? Why would she want to go to the other side of the country for a university program that she could take right here in our community, times two?

But she wants this. I had seen her happiness over the first two acceptance letters, but this was something more. This was pure joy. Pure joy at the thought of leaving her hometown, and me, to go to school somewhere so far away that I would need to take an airplane just to visit her. It hit me at that moment that I was going to be alone, utterly alone, rattling around by myself in this big house. The human equivalent of a ball in a pinball game. Tilt. No penthouse condo, no Ryan, and now, no Sara.

"We were thinking of going next week," Sara was saying.

"What? I didn't catch that."

"Olivia and I, we're thinking about flying down to the university next week. To tour the campus and get oriented a little bit with the city." Sara was talking so fast now, it was taking all my focus just to keep up with the sentence.

"When exactly were you planning to ask me about this? I mean, since when do you plan to fly to the other side of the country by yourself without even talking to me about it?" It came out all at once, almost like a blast. A blast of anger, an explosion of pent-up frustration. What the hell was going on here? When did she even have time to make these plans with Olivia, or Olivia and her parents? Olivia's parents were okay with this?

"Congratulations? I think that must have been what you meant to say?"

"Yes, of course, I am proud of you for getting into all three universities that you applied to. Congratulations, Sara. That is really quite a feat. But what about the two local universities?"

"Mom, I have had my heart set on the University of British Columbia. Although I didn't really think I had any real chance. They have the most sought-after psychology program in the country."

"That's great, and I am happy for you. But I don't understand why it would make a huge difference in your ultimate career as a psychologist. No matter where you choose to go to school, your degree will be the same."

"Yes, I would graduate with the same degree. But the fact remains that this"—she waved her acceptance letter in the air—"is the university I've been dreaming about being lucky enough to be accepted to."

"You have time to think about it before you make any rash decisions."

"Rash decisions? Any other mother would be dancing around and looking to call everyone they know to brag. But not my mom. No, she is too busy trying to

241

push me into doing exactly what she wants. To keep me here, living in Haven with you. I don't know what happened between you and Ryan, and I was giving you your privacy, so I didn't ask. But you have been moody and upset for a couple of weeks now. And you are allowing that to colour how you see this opportunity for me."

"Excuse me, but this has nothing to do with my relationship with Ryan. It has to do with you, going across the entire country to take a course that you could take right in our backyard."

"Well, if it doesn't have anything to do with you and Ryan breaking up, then I have no choice but to think that this reaction is just you trying to control me. You are trying your damnedest to keep me living here with you, keep me your little girl forever. If you haven't noticed, I have grown up. I'm not a little girl anymore. I'm eighteen, I'm an adult, and I get to make my own decisions. Whether you like that fact or not!"

"Well, since you are an adult and you don't have to listen to me anymore, then I guess you don't need me to cover the cost of your education at this fancy university or the cost of the airplane ticket to British Columbia next week either!"

"Ugh! I can't believe you are being like this. I have been putting away half of my paycheck at the drugstore ever since I started working there. I will pay for my own damn ticket! I am going with Olivia to British Columbia whether you like it or not." Flushed with anger, Sara turned on her heel and headed to the stairs. When she reached the first step, she turned back to look at me once more. "Dad would have been so proud of me. Dad would have congratulated me." Then, with tears beginning to roll down her cheeks, she turned and took the stairs two at a time.

I was left standing in the hall feeling two conflicting emotions, anger and deep sadness. Deep sadness because she was right; John would have been so proud and excited for her.

I THOUGHT about calling in sick, but then I remembered that I own the café. So there was that, and the fact that I hadn't made any arrangements with Katie to do the early morning baking. I had hardly slept, tossing and turning between fits of anger and depression. Well, maybe not depression. Maybe more like feeling sorry for myself. I found out that even a seventy-dollar concealer can't touch the dark circles under your eyes from not sleeping. I did the best I could with makeup, and the best hair updo I could muster. I put on my favourite sweater, which hugged me in all the right places and was so soft it kind of felt like I was wearing a teddy bear. Just the thought of having a teddy bear with me at all times felt comforting, and I needed all the comfort that I could get this morning.

"WHAT HAPPENED TO YOU?" Katie asked as she came into the kitchen to drop off her stuff before starting for the day.

"Why? Do I have an explosion of flour that I can't see?"

"No, you look like you could take someone's head off if they looked at you wrong."

"Thanks so much. I had a terrible night's sleep, and Sara and I are fighting."

The door chimed, telling us that the first customer of the day had arrived.

"I will serve whoever that is." She pointed at me. "You. Stay here. And I mean it! We will talk when I return."

I was still stewing over being forced to stay in my own damn kitchen. By a five-foot-nothing demon. I mean, I love Katie... but she could be one scary lady.

"The mean customers are all gone," she cooed while perching on the table, staring down at me. "Now that Mommy made those bad, bad customers go away. Tell Mommy what's wrong."

"Katie, do not try and be cute with me. I am not in the mood."

"This I can tell. So, you and Sara are fighting. Well, she is a teenage girl. I mean... this is going to happen from time to time. Two stubborn women butting heads."

"She wants to go to university across the entire damn country! She is going to leave me, Ryan already left me, and The Penthouses sold out before I could buy a condo. I feel angry! And... shit on! I mean, what the actual hell?"

"You never told me about The Penthouses being sold out. That's a bummer for sure, but I know for a fact that they are planning on building at least two phases maybe three. So, you may have missed this phase... but that doesn't mean that you can't purchase a condo in phase two."

"In two years, minimum!" I began to rhythmically bang my head against the table.

"That's it! I am putting my foot down." She hopped off the table and dramatically stomped her foot on the floor. "You are taking the rest of the day off."

"But..." I started to say something in response when she cut me off.

"No buts. You are going home, shopping, or to the wine bar, or the spa, come to think of it. Anyway, the point being, you are going to spend the rest of the day anywhere but here." She then turned and started to head back out front at the sound of the door chiming again. She turned back to look at me just as she reached the kitchen door and pointed one finger directly at me. "And don't even think about coming back here until you have had some sleep and you no longer have a black cloud floating over your head." She then sailed through the door, but I could hear her last comment float from around the corner. "Honest to God! The look on your face today could curdle the milk."

Curdle the milk? Fine, I could use a day off, I decided. I haven't seen Beth in a couple of weeks. She and her dad were due a visit and I could really use a shoulder to cry... no, vent upon.

Chapter Thirty-Two

Beth did not look as frazzled as she had the last time I visited. She smiled widely and welcomed me inside. I could see her dad sitting at the kitchen table, and he called me over as I tossed my purse on the front bench.

"Other One," he called. "Come and see my latest project."

I was impressed to see a huge puzzle, three-quarters of the way finished. It was made from some of the tiniest puzzle pieces, and the puzzle itself was a landscape with a lot of blue skies.

"Wow, looking good, Mr. Martin. I would never even have attempted that puzzle—too much sky."

"The sky is the best part," Gus said, beaming. "I like the challenge of it."

I was happy to see Mr. Martin dressed, out of bed, and generally looking more like himself.

"You look good, by the way. How are you feeling these days?"

"Great, thanks. I feel more like myself every day."

I FOUND Beth in the living room, setting two large glasses of white wine on the coffee table.

"It's only ten in the morning." I gave Beth a mock horrified look.

"More for me then." Beth grabbed the glass closest to me and set it beside hers.

I grabbed my glass back. "Not so fast. What I drink at Beth's at ten in the morning stays at Beth's... at ten in the morning. Right?" I gave her my best shit-eating grin and took a big gulp of my "breakfast wine."

"You looked like you had something on your mind. So, have a seat and tell me what's wrong."

I filled Beth in on everything, and she listened, refilling our wine glasses mid-way through my stories of how my life was going to hell.

"Don't kill the messenger, but I think that, knowing Sara... I think her reasoning behind wanting to go to British Columbia University includes simply being excited to have reached her goal of acceptance there. That and being able to go and live in a beautiful, exciting, new city with her very best friend. And I am willing to bet that this has absolutely nothing to do with being far away from you. Sara loves you. I know it, and you know it."

I nodded in reply. Deep down I knew I was allowing myself and my carefully constructed plans to get in the way of seeing the situation from Sara's point of view.

"Now, that condominium. I meant it when I said that you shouldn't shortchange the joy you get from living in such a beautiful house. Your own private yard, no noisy neighbours fighting on the other side of your shared wall. Being able to spin around in your living room without touching every wall. I miss my house every single day."

Before I could reply to that, Beth continued.

"And as far as Ryan is concerned... sounds like you dodged a bullet there. I mean, any man that would be so stupid as to cheat on you doesn't deserve you. What excuses did he give when you confronted him?"

"I haven't confronted him... yet," I mumbled.

"Why not? He's avoiding you, isn't he? Coward, typical!" Beth was beginning to get visibly angry.

"It's not like that. He has been trying ever since that night to talk to me. He has left voice messages and texts and shown up at my home and the café. . . ."

"Reminds me of Chris after I caught him and Candice having sex in her backyard. That was after telling me that he would just pop over and help Candice with a blocked sink. I mean, that alone should have alerted me that he was lying. Since when did he ever fix anything around our house? He was about as useful as a knitted condom."

"Well, I don't think it's quite the same. I mean, I just saw the text messages about a kiss..."

But Beth was on a roll by this time, and once she started rolling down this particular hill there was no stopping her.

"He kept on saying we just needed to talk it through. Do you want to know the worst part?"

I don't know why she framed that as a question because she had no intention of letting me answer.

"The worst part is that, for months, I had been noticing our sex life become increasingly infrequent. I didn't know why. He suddenly didn't have much of a sex drive. I would ask him if he wanted to make love, and he would always have an excuse like he had a terrible headache or his mind was on a problem that his boss had dumped on him from work. I tried to be understanding, but I was becoming more and more frustrated. So much so that I confided in Candice about our lack of a sex life. And she had the audacity to advise me to buy some sexy lingerie to try and get the old excitement back. Oh... and cook him a special meal and serve it to him wearing an apron with nothing else underneath. And the heartbreaking part is... I did! I bought new sexy lingerie, and I made him dinner served with nothing on except an apron. Of course, it didn't fix anything. Because the problem wasn't with me, the problem was with my husband sleeping with Candice! How she must have laughed with Chris about her suggestions."

She stopped for just a moment to catch her breath. "He wasn't sleeping with me, his own wife... because... he wanted to be faithful to Candice. How pathetic is that?"

She had been looking down into her lap, lost in thought for a minute or two, when she suddenly seemed to remember that I was there. "I am so sorry. I've done it again, haven't I? You came here wanting a shoulder to cry on, and instead of being your support, I made it all about myself. I feel terrible. My therapist says, 'everyone has problems, and it isn't a competition. And if it was a competition, would I really want to win?' I believe you told me something similar not long ago."

"I like your therapist already—'smart minds think alike.' That's good advice. And Beth, don't worry about it. You've really made me think about a few things in a way that I didn't before." I reached over and squeezed her shoulder. "I love you. You are talented and beautiful, fun and giving. But you're putting too much of your precious energy into rehashing the past and not putting enough into building something new. Something that has nothing to do with Chris, or Candy—something just for you. Something great."

WHEN I ARRIVED home just after noon, I saw an unfamiliar hatchback in the driveway. As I started up the porch stairs, I noticed that Sandy had been waiting for me on my porch swing.

"Evie, I hope you don't mind. But I needed to talk to you, and you'd gone home early. So I asked Katie for your address."

"That's okay, Sandy," I said as I reached the front door and punched in the passcode. "Come on in then. I'll put on a pot of coffee, and we can talk."

Sandy seemed uncomfortable; she was moving in an almost mechanical, slightly rigid way, and she kept fidgeting with her necklace.

"What did you need to talk about?"

"It's about Ryan." She looked at my expression. "I

know that it's none of my business. But please, just let me say this and then if you never want to talk about it again, I will honour that."

I nodded in response.

"Ryan has been really upset, and all I could get out of him was that he was trying to get hold of you, but you had stopped answering his calls. He didn't want to talk anymore about it, and at first I didn't want to press him. But it's been a while now, and he has been so upset and moody that, when I saw him last night, I decided to press him about it. He told me he had been out to dinner with you and had a really good time. But when he left the table, he thought you must have seen a text come through his phone from Lena and misinterpreted it."

I interrupted her. "You know what? It's fine. I mean, Ryan is allowed to hang out with his friends. But I draw the line when he is kissing them. Especially when he cancels a dinner with Sara and me to do it!"

Sandy was taking a breath and I knew she was waiting for me to pause so she could get in with her counterpoint. Instead of letting her butt in, I decided to get it all out.

"It makes sense." That statement seemed to surprise Sandy. "Lena is closer to Ryan's age, and she could give Ryan the family he's always wanted. Ryan told me about his marriage breakdown. It sounded like having a baby was a big part of that. I have already had my family, and at this point in my life, I have closed the door to having more children. So... maybe it's actually for the best?"

"Wow. There has been a lot of misunderstanding going on here."

This time I tried to butt in. "Sandy..."

Sandy held up her hand. "You had your turn; now let me have mine. Ryan told me about the kiss. You need to know that Lena has been a good friend of Ryan's for years. And I always thought Lena wanted something more than friendship, but that was only on Lena's part. Ryan just wanted to be friends. Ryan said that Lena was very drunk, slurring on the phone and asking for his help. When he got to her place she was crying, and Ryan was trying to calm her down. He said he sat beside her on the sofa and was trying to get out of her what had upset her. She told him she'd been in love with him for a long time and that she wanted to let him know before it was too late. And then he said she suddenly just leaned over and kissed him. He told me he was stunned and he didn't kiss her back. He just told her he was grateful for their friendship and how much it meant to him. But then he told her he only felt friendship for her and was in love with you. She didn't take that news well, but she didn't start crying again, and after getting a glass of water and Tylenol into her, he left. The next day, however, she seemed to have memories of only part of the evening. She remembered the kiss but not the conversation with Ryan, saying that he only wanted to stay friends and nothing more."

"Oh." I was searching my brain for a proper response, but it seemed frozen. "Oh, well... that explains a few things." I opened my mouth to say something more, but when nothing more came out, I slowly closed my mouth again.

"And as far as Ryan wanting to have a family of his

own... I think you only have part of the story. It's true that they were having fertility problems. But did you know that the fertility problems were found to be Ryan's? The specialist told him that he wouldn't be able to father a child. Ryan said he had come to terms with it and was talking to Deb about adoption. But Deb wasn't interested in adoption. She wanted to have a baby of her own. Ryan wasn't sure he wanted to go ahead with a sperm donor. And then... well, you know how the story ends. With Deb pregnant from her affair and super happy about it. She left Ryan without a backward glance." Sandy paused for a moment.

"You need to call Ryan and talk this out with him. I watched the two of you at the wedding, and I don't think I have ever seen him so happy. I think you two could be so good together. And speaking for myself, I would love to see you at all our family functions."

Everything was clicking into place all of a sudden.

"Thank you so much, Sandy. Can I ask you for a favour?"

Chapter Thirty-Three

Sara and I had a long talk that evening; we shared some raised voices, a lot of tears, and in the end, some big bear hugs. I told Sara that I had been so wrapped up in everything I felt I had lost; that I was trying to hold on tight to everything I had left—too tight. Sara's anger melted after that, and she told me she was going to miss me. But she wanted to make plans with me so she could come back to visit every chance she could. She also wanted me to go with her to British Columbia this summer to see where she would be living and going to school.

We talked about The Penthouses and how I was going to have to put myself on the list for phase two and hold tight for the time being. Sara pointed out that, with the basement almost finished, I could soon rent it out as an apartment.

"With the money you'd get for rent, you can hire someone to cut the grass, shovel the snow, and clean the house if you want. Dad would love how the basement has turned out, wouldn't he? He would have loved the antique touches of the sconces and the fireplace; it almost looks like he had finished it himself."

"You're right, he would have loved it. And I do have a lot of options. I need to take a breath and figure out what I want. I just know that I want you to be happy. No matter where in the country that takes you or how far away from me, we will always find a way to stay connected."

THE FOLLOWING day I woke up early and started phase one of my grand plan. I quickly dressed and headed to the farmers' market to pick out the freshest produce, then off to the butcher for the perfect cut of prime rib.

After I got home from shopping, I crammed the food into the refrigerator and headed upstairs to prepare for the day.

I HAD CALLED Katie the night before and asked if she could take over the baking at the café this morning. She seemed delighted to help me out, especially after discovering why.

"No problem. Absolutely, I will come in and do the baking, and I can hold the fort for the day. You go, girl. Go and get your man!" She was squealing with excitement over the phone at this point. "I knew you two were perfect for each other! I just knew it." She sighed longingly. "What are you going to wear, by the way? Do you want to have a look at my closet? You can borrow anything you want."

"No need, Katie, thanks though. I have everything I need here once I find it. I think it's in the kitchen somewhere. Now I have to go to bed. Tomorrow, I put my plan into action."

"Wait! What?"

I TOOK my time getting ready, took a long, relaxing milk bath, and watched a video on YouTube to help me get my hair into that elusive messy-bun look that I found so hard to achieve.

Downstairs, I was pulling the kitchen apart, looking for something that a girlfriend had given me years ago as a joke birthday present. I finally found it crammed in a too-high cupboard that I generally reserved for kitchen items I rarely used, like the extra-large roasting pan and the ice cream maker. It was just as I remembered it. It was perfect.

I WAS ready and waiting when Paul and David arrived for the day.

"Mrs. Jones, I mean Evie, I'm surprised to see you here." Paul almost leaped back when he opened the front door to see me standing there waiting for him.

"Hi, Paul, hi, David. Come on in and get ready for the day. And then, I'd like it if you would join me upstairs. I'll put on a fresh pot of coffee for us, and I would like to ask the two of you for a favour."

.   .   .

I HAD JUST FINISHED SETTING the table and lighting the candles when I heard Ryan's truck pull into the driveway. I had brought over some of my good china and two tall crystal flutes for the champagne I had picked out. The table looked beautiful if I do say so myself. I used my fancy cloth napkins, and there was a vase filled with a colourful bouquet in the centre. Paul and David had agreed to help me by keeping Ryan busy with a fake problem at my house. They seemed flattered to be asked to be part of my plan. I transferred the special dinner I had precooked over to Ryan's house just before Paul texted him to request his assistance with a problem at my house that was, of course, of their own making. I had arranged for Sandy to be waiting at Ryan's house to let me in with her key, and she had her phone with her at all times. David and Paul had agreed to text Sandy if they were unable to keep Ryan at my house for long enough. Sandy would then take over, keeping Ryan occupied outside of his house until the arranged time of six o'clock.

I was shaking with nerves because, if this didn't go well, it could end up being very embarrassing for me. But as Katie had once told me, love is always worth taking a chance on. And I was going big or going home, as they say.

I looked down and smoothed my killer apron; it was just as I had remembered it: with black and white ruffled polka-dot trim and a gorgeous moody red floral fabric. It was made in a fifties pin-up style, and it was sexy as hell. I checked that the bow was still properly tied around my waist. It was important that the apron looked just right because it was the sum total of what I was wearing. Outside of my killer red high heels, of course. Now I had never eaten or served a meal naked before—well, almost naked, anyway. But Beth's story had given me an idea for a grand gesture, one to top all grand gestures.

RYAN'S KEY could be heard in the door, and I waited at his kitchen table, shaking like a leaf but attempting to look calm.

"Hello? Is somebody in here?"

"I'm in the kitchen."

Ryan came around the corner and dropped his lunch bag to the floor with a loud thump when he saw me. He stood there silently for a moment with a completely blank expression.

"What's going on?" he finally managed to say.

"Well, I'm making a grand gesture, to apologize for shutting you out and not letting you tell me your side of the story."

"I know what you think happened with Lena, but you're wrong. I would never cheat on you. I've fallen in love with you."

"I know that... now. I was so sure you would want Lena over me, especially since I had seen her mooning over you that night at Archie's. And I'd been feeling . . . a bit insecure about your marriage failing over not being able to start a family. I didn't want to take that experience away, especially when I knew how important it was to you."

"My marriage failed because Deb cheated on me and stopped communicating with me. There are so many ways to make a family, and Deb just wasn't willing to look at it that way. I don't think that just because you can't have your own biological children it means that you can't find other ways to be a parent. I want to get to know Sara better, because I want to be part of her life. I know that I'll never replace her father, but I would love to, one day, become her stepfather. And I know that is down the road a little way, but I want you to know what I am thinking. I don't want any more misunderstandings to come between us."

He walked around the table and swept me up into his arms.

"I love what you're wearing, by the way. Or, should I say, *not* wearing?" He kissed me softly and let one hand drift down my back and cup my behind. "Now, I know that you have worked really hard on this supper. And it smells amazing, by the way. But... I am hoping it will still taste amazing cold. Because I am going to take you upstairs to my bedroom right now and show you a grand gesture of my own."

And I had no objections.

Epilogue

The morning sun woke me, and I rolled over to find myself alone in the bed. I looked around Ryan's bedroom—well, actually, our bedroom now—and didn't see any sign of him.

Ryan walked into the bedroom with two steaming mugs of coffee a few minutes later, just in time to catch me stretching lazily in bed.

"Oh, how I love a man that brings me coffee in bed," I said as I grabbed the offered mug.

Ryan sat on the bed and leaned over to kiss me. "Good morning, Sunshine. How did you sleep?"

"Like a baby. It is such a revelation not to have to get up at the crack of dawn every morning."

I now had Katie doing the morning baking every other day. She had taken over happily, and she had been coming up with her own twists on my recipes, to great success. Her specialty drinks had become part of the regular menu because they were such a roaring success, and I very happily gave her that corresponding raise.

I don't live in The Penthouses, but I don't miss that fact after selling my house for over the asking price, in part because of the beautiful in-law suite. When I moved in with Ryan, we decided to use some of the money from the house sale to buy a condo in British Columbia, near the university. Sara and Olivia live there instead of living in residence at the University, and there is an extra bedroom, reserved for me or Ryan and me. I go over to visit Sara every other month, and Ryan comes with me when he can. Sara has a bedroom here at our townhouse, so she can come and visit us here in Haven on school holidays and, fingers-crossed, maybe for the summer. I must admit, Sara has really come into her own at university, and it has been a pleasure to watch.

"Now—since I don't have any job sites that need my presence this morning... how about we start the day with a grand gesture?"

I smiled into my mug of coffee.

"Who am I to turn down a grand gesture?" I put my mug down on the bedside table and turned towards Ryan's warm embrace.

Coming Soon...

Can't get enough of Evie's Haven?
Stay tuned for Beth's Haven,
the second book in the Haven series!

Acknowledgments

My profound thanks go out first and foremost to my husband and my kids. Your belief in me gave me the strength to keep going, even when I doubted myself. You are the very first people on the planet to call me a writer and an author, even when I didn't feel like I truly was. So thank you, thank you Rob, Justin, Nick and Linda! And to Matthew, I love you and think of you always!

I had the pleasure and privilege of working with the world's most supportive and talented publisher, Barbara Storey of *Storeylines Press*. You were willing to take a chance on me, and I will forever be grateful that you did. Your cooperative and hands-on approach must be why you have been called "The Book Doula.'" Thank you!

To my best friends, you know who you are! Thank you for being the very first people to read and champion my work. Thank you for being my cheerleaders and for having my back when I was having a bad day. Everyone should have friends like you!

Thank you to all my friends and family who are too numerous to name here; all of you have been so supportive of me. I will happily sign a copy for each and every one of you, although, for my family... some scenes might need to be redacted. So we can still make eye contact at the next family meal! :)

Last of all, I would like to thank my readers. I hope you enjoy my debut novel, and that you feel I have dealt with some of the more sensitive topics with the respect and understanding they deserve.

About the Author

Lisa Plaice was born, raised and still lives in southern Ontario, Canada. She loves her family, sewing projects that are sometimes inappropriate, and making people laugh. When she isn't working at her day job, reading, writing, or sewing, she is probably singing (badly)  to her Grand-dogger Stella. Her goal in writing this, her first novel, is to help readers escape and live in the charming town of Haven for a time, and laugh, cry, and ultimately cheer on Evie to find her happy ending.

facebook.com/profile.php_id=61553675340043

instagram.com/plaicelisa

Manufactured by Amazon.ca
Bolton, ON

38266171R00162